Enrollment Form

☐ *Yes!* I WANT TO BE A *Privileged Woman.*
Enclosed is one *PAGES & PRIVILEGES™* Proof of
Purchase from any Harlequin or Silhouette book currently for
sale in stores (Proofs of Purchase are found on the back pages
of books) and the store cash register receipt. Please enroll me
in *PAGES & PRIVILEGES™.* Send my Welcome Kit and FREE
Gifts – and activate my FREE benefits – immediately.

More great gifts and benefits to come.

NAME (please print)
_____

ADDRESS _____ APT. NO _____

CITY _____ STATE _____ ZIP/POSTAL CODE _____

PROOF OF PURCHASE
ONLY

**NO CLUB!
NO COMMITMENT!**
*Just one purchase brings
you great Free Gifts and
Benefits!*

Please allow 6-8 weeks for delivery. Quantities are limited. We reserve the right to
substitute items. Enroll before October 31, 1995 and receive one full year of benefits.

Name of store where this book was purchased_____

Date of purchase_____

Type of store:
☐ Bookstore   ☐ Supermarket   ☐ Drugstore
☐ Dept. or discount store (e.g. K-Mart or Walmart)
☐ Other (specify)_____

Which Harlequin or Silhouette series do you usually read?
_____

Complete and mail with one Proof of Purchase and store receipt to:
U.S.: *PAGES & PRIVILEGES™,* P.O. Box 1960, Danbury, CT 06813-1960
Canada: *PAGES & PRIVILEGES™,* 49-6A The Donway West, P.O. 813,
     North York, ON M3C 2E8

▼ DETACH HERE AND MAIL TODAY! ▼

I wish he'd kiss me,
Kayla thought.

Why didn't he? Why didn't he just give in and do it? Kiss me, please!

The air between them quivered, with attraction, with longing. And with control. Matt swallowed hard and dragged his gaze from hers.

No, they wouldn't kiss. Couldn't kiss. Not now. Something between them had changed.

Dear Reader,

No slogan could be more fitting for my story,
The Best Man, than the one that now graces the covers
of Harlequin Romance—**"Dare to Dream."**

My heroine, Kayla Brayton, attains the man of her
dreams but only after heeding her own needs and
aspirations. It isn't easy—she's faced with reversing the
entire course of her life—but her true happiness isn't
possible otherwise.

I firmly believe this—that a person must be happy
in herself first. This often means looking beyond
limitations to what seems impossible—dreaming—
but the rewards are beyond measure: romance perhaps
with a wonderful man or, if one is truly blessed, a
romance with life itself.

I hope that you enjoy *The Best Man,* and may your
life be filled with happy dreaming.

Shannon Waverly

The Best Man
Shannon Waverly

Harlequin Books

TORONTO • NEW YORK • LONDON
AMSTERDAM • PARIS • SYDNEY • HAMBURG
STOCKHOLM • ATHENS • TOKYO • MILAN
MADRID • WARSAW • BUDAPEST • AUCKLAND

ISBN 0-373-03380-X

THE BEST MAN

First North American Publication 1995.

Copyright © 1995 by Kathleen Shannon.

This edition published by arrangement with Harlequin Books S.A.

® and TM are trademarks of the publisher. Trademarks indicated with ® are registered in the United States Patent and Trademark Office, the Canadian Trade Marks Office and in other countries.

Printed in U.S.A.

CHAPTER ONE

KAYLA remembered Matt Reed as a handsome, self-assured twenty-one-year-old, and she fully expected to find him a handsome, self-assured thirty-one-year-old. But when she saw him step out of his office, laughing at whatever the client with him was saying, she realized that if she'd contemplated him for a thousand years, she still wouldn't have fully conjured up the man who stood before her now.

Simultaneously, she thought, *The photo in* The Bostonian *didn't do him justice.* The previous year she'd come across an article about him in the regional magazine, which she'd faithfully subscribed to through all five of her moves the past five years. He'd made the magazine's annual Most Eligible Bachelor List, a choice based on looks, personality and, above all, success. Not that he hadn't looked handsome in the photo. He had. But only now did Kayla understand what the columnist had meant when she'd written, "When you meet Matt Reed, you only hope you can find your voice."

It wasn't exactly his dark good looks that were making Kayla forget to breathe, although those were certainly distracting enough. It was something more—the way the very climate in the room had changed when he'd entered it.

She let out her breath very slowly and, blinking, turned her gaze aside. This was hardly a good way to begin their meeting.

Another deep, slow breath—and she thought she'd put her reaction into some sort of perspective. Her heart wasn't racing because of Matt Reed per se. Good Lord, she was practically engaged. Rather, she was responding to the seriousness of her mission here and her sudden realization that Matt was not a foe to take lightly.

That was it. Sure.

That, and *maybe* some lingering vulnerability she still carried around in her personality from her teenage years, some murky emotional memory that had no place or meaning in the present.

He said goodbye to his client and placed a folder on the receptionist's desk, a curve of polished granite that looked more like a modern sculpture than a piece of furniture. The decor at Reed and Associates, the accounting and financial services firm that Matt owned, was bold, strong, sophisticated. Kayla imagined a client felt prosperous just stepping into such an assertive environment.

After checking his phone messages, he slanted a look Kayla's way. She was seated beside a contemporary-style grandfather clock and just to the left of a computer screen set into the wall displaying the latest Dow Jones. The clock was a Brayton's, and while she and Matt Reed eyed each other it began to chime the half hour. Twelve-thirty.

"Ms. Brayton?" he said, as punctual as the time-piece. His tone was merely polite, as if she were a stranger to him, and from the way his slightly puzzled eyes kept moving over her, she thought maybe she was. Maybe he'd totally forgotten her.

Caught somewhere between pique and relief, she got to her feet, gathered up her purse and surreptitiously checked her reflection in the glass door of the clock. All she could really discern, however, was that her blond hair, swirled up in its customary French twist, still appeared neat . . . and she still looked anxiety-ridden.

Making an effort to smooth the furrow over her worried blue eyes, she turned and followed him into his office. Passing him at the door, she gauged he'd grown another couple of inches since they'd last met, making him six-one or six-two. He'd become heavier, too, the fluid lines of his Armani suit doing nothing to hide the solid breadth of his shoulders or the muscularity of his thighs.

"Have a seat," he offered, touching the back of a leather chair as he rounded a massive desk in front of a wall of glass.

Kayla was so taken with the spectacular view out the window—all the glass and metallic flash of Boston's financial district, sharpened under the cold light of a February sun—that when she sat, she came down on the arm of the chair and almost tumbled.

Finding the seat, she straightened the slim navy skirt of her Chanel suit and chided herself for blushing. For heaven's sake, she did business with men like Matt Reed all the time. She had no reason to feel intimidated in his presence.

She lifted her chin, gave him a direct stare—and then swallowed uncomfortably. No, no one she did business with was quite like Matt Reed. A few *might* be as self-possessed and successful, but not at his age.

"Well, if it isn't Kayla Brayton," he said. Matt's voice was a deep slow rumble as he settled back in his chair, his gaze running over her again.

So he does remember me, she thought.

A hint of a smile touched his lips as he added, "I hardly recognized you."

Kayla squeezed the strap of her purse. She knew she'd changed considerably from the awkward sixteen-year-old he'd escorted to her high school Christmas dance ten years ago. But she also knew she wasn't a beauty, and she wasn't about to think he'd meant anything by that comment except, simply, that she'd changed.

"How long has it been?"

She shrugged her eyebrows. "Nine years? Ten?" As if she didn't know.

He whistled softly between his teeth, his eyes never leaving her face. "So, how are you, Kayla?"

She worked at keeping her gaze as unwavering as his. "Very well. Very busy. And you?" she asked briskly, even while soaking up the details of his appearance.

His hair was as thick as ever, straight, coarse and nearly black, the attractive and undoubtedly expensive cut framing a face that had lost its boyishness to become a collection of no-nonsense angles—wide, intelligent brow, rawboned cheeks, straight nose, chiseled jaw. Even his mouth seemed to have hardened and matured. Oh, but his eyes, those steady, penetrating gray eyes. They hit like a tumble down an elevator shaft.

"I'm fine," he replied, again with that slightly condescending amusement in his voice. He appeared relaxed, but Kayla sensed a certain watchfulness in him, as well. A Bach fugue played from some invisible source, adding a subtle aura of calculation and precision to the room.

He stared at her, silent and waiting, until she finally said, "I imagine you're wondering why I'm here."

"Yes, I am curious," he returned smoothly. "Although considering the recent events involving my father and your grandmother, I think I can safely assume you're not here to explore mutual funds. Am I right?" His watchfulness sharpened to a fine, coiled tension.

The question needed no answer. Kayla crossed her legs and smoothed her skirt, thinking back to the phone call she'd received from her father two days earlier that had apprised her of the situation. It had been a Wednesday evening, she'd been bone-weary from work, and the last thing she'd needed was the news that her grandmother had run off with the family accountant, Philip Reed. According to her father, Ruth and Philip had managed to make arrangements, pack their bags and slip away without a single person catching on.

When Kayla asked where they'd gone, her father's answer had floored her. The Bahamas? She couldn't imagine her grandmother in the Bahamas. Ruth Brayton had never liked beaches. She'd liked taking vacations even less.

What really worried Kayla, though, was the fact that Ruth was seventy-one years old. She'd had a heart attack the previous summer. She was on a special diet, a special regimen of sleep and exercise. Her doctors were in Boston, her friends, her family. Being in the Bahamas made absolutely no sense.

The situation was especially worrisome because Ruth refused to tell anyone in the family where she was exactly, and there were any number of islands she could be on.

Kayla blinked, bringing the present—and Matt Reed—into focus. "I'm sorry to bring a personal family matter to your workplace," she said with professional crispness, "but I wanted to speak with you as soon as possible."

Matt Reed shrugged off her apology while pressing the intercom. "Sara, will you find out what's keeping lunch?"

The tinny voice of his receptionist replied that the cart was just coming off the elevator.

He sat back. "I hope you don't mind if I combine lunch with our meeting. This was the only free time I had today to see you. You called at such short notice."

Whether Kayla minded or not, the door opened and a waiter pushed a food cart into the office, going directly to a conference table.

"Will you join me?" Matt got to his feet.

"No, thank you. I had a late breakfast." That wasn't true, but Kayla's stomach had been jumping so distressfully since her father's phone call she doubted she'd be able to swallow a single bite.

After sketching the predicament, Lloyd Brayton had asked his daughter to fly home. There was more to the problem than he cared to discuss on the phone.

"When?" she'd asked.

"As soon as possible. Tomorrow would be good."

For some reason, the distance between Chicago and Boston seemed never to have registered with him. Nor had the fact that Kayla was an extremely busy person with complicated responsibilities. She couldn't just pick up and go.

But because they were talking about her grandmother, Kayla did exactly that. She was on an eastbound plane the very next morning, head pounding, wondering what she could possibly do to help, trying not to dwell on the fact her father had forgotten all about her recent trip to San Francisco where she hoped to open the next Brayton Clockworks.

Matt Reed pulled out a chair for her at the table. "I have to tell you, Kayla, I find your coming here...interesting." He settled opposite her and lifted the cover off a chafing dish. "After meeting with your father and your brother, I really expected their attorney to be next. I didn't think they'd send the baby of the family."

She fought back a wave of resentment, reminding herself that arguing would be counterproductive. Her father and Gordon had gone that route and got nowhere for their efforts.

"I just flew in yesterday."

"Oh, that's right. Your grandmother mentioned something about your living out west."

"Chicago," she corrected. "I haven't lived in Boston for five years."

"Hmm. I didn't think I'd seen you around."

As if he'd been looking, she thought ruefully. Being her escort had probably been the absolute low point of his dating career, and why her brother thought it gave her an edge was beyond her.

Matt looked at her inquiringly. "Are you sure you won't join me?"

The uncovered serving dishes offered an array of crisp steamed vegetables, slices of lean turkey, herb-seasoned pasta, whole wheat rolls and fresh fruit, while bottles of mineral water and assorted vitamins formed a centerpiece. A power lunch if she ever saw one.

She glanced at her watch. She ought to eat. Doing two things at once saved time, and if Kayla Brayton was anything, it was a master of efficiency.

Apparently so was Matt Reed. His office was filled with a dizzying array of electronic wonders, and through a half-open door to an adjoining room, she glimpsed an impressive collection of exercise equipment, along with additional phones and a TV and VCR. Files were strewn on a massage table.

With a sigh of concession, she spooned a small portion of vegetables onto a plate.

"So, why *are* you here? You still haven't told me," Matt said, filling his own plate. "Have you heard from your grandmother? Has something new developed that I don't know about?"

"Uh...no. Nothing new. Basically I'm just worried about her, Matt. Really worried. We all are. That's why I came to see you, to tell you she isn't well. I'm not sure you fully understand how grave her condition is." That was the approach her father and Gordon had suggested she take—no threats, just concern for Ruth's health and an affirmation of their love for her. Maybe if *she* told him, they'd said, it would sound more moving.

"How grave is it?" Matt asked evenly, reaching for a roll.

"How grave?"

"Yes. What are the details?" He waited, watching her. Challenge glinted in his gray eyes.

She poured a glass of water and took too big a swallow. It hurt all the way down. "Well, the condition that led to her heart attack last summer hasn't gone away," she said. "It's under control and possibly on the mend, but unless she remains under her doctor's close supervision, she could have another attack at any time."

"Really?" One dark eyebrow lifted, making her feel like a student who'd just bluffed her way through a recitation.

Still, she jutted her chin and boldly answered, "Yes."

The eyebrow rose higher.

Damn. Why hadn't she prepared more carefully? Why hadn't she anticipated Matt would be a man who was used to fully researched reports? She should've called her grandmother's physician and come armed with proper facts and figures. She could've dazzled him if only she'd thought this through.

"And what exactly do you want from me?" he asked coolly.

His indifference offended her, yet she managed a smile and said, "I understand that you know where she is. When she phoned my father last week to assure him she was all right, she said we should call you if any emergency arose and you'd relay the message." The family suspected that Matt not only knew where Ruth was but that he'd orchestrated the entire getaway, as well—plane reservations, accommodations, everything. But because it remained a suspicion, Kayla kept it to herself.

"That's correct. Is there a message you want me to pass on?"

"No. What I'm wondering is, would you be kind enough to share the address with me?"

Without missing a beat Matt replied, "I don't think so."

Under the table, Kayla's nails bit into her palms. "How about the phone number, then? That'll do."

He looked right at her, every trace of amusement gone from his eyes now, and asked, "Why?"

"I...I want to talk to her, make sure she's all right."

"And?"

"And what?"

"If you're so concerned about her health, surely you'll want to do more than just talk on the phone."

"No, really, that's all." She looked aside, knowing that was not all. Her father had got her to agree to one more measure.

"Then why did you ask for the address first?"

Her stomach was knotting in anger, at him for being so difficult, at herself for pussyfooting. "You're right. You're absolutely right. I want to visit her, too. I need to see for myself that she's okay." In her experience she'd always found honesty to be the most productive policy.

"And if she isn't?"

"I'm hoping to convince her to come back to Boston where her physicians are." There, she'd said it. All her cards were on the table. Well, almost all.

Matt stared at her an uncomfortably long time. "Are you sure her health is the only thing that's got you worried?" His deep voice vibrated with insinuation.

She caught the insinuation and her eyes widened. "Excuse me?"

He shrugged unapologetically. "Ruth *is* a wealthy woman."

"Her money has nothing to do with my concern."

"How refreshing." His tone was cynical. Kayla wondered how she'd ended up on the defensive when *he* was the one in the wrong.

He glanced impatiently at his watch. "Kayla, I suggest we cut to the chase. I have another appointment at one."

Her breath came in short, shallow jerks. "What do you mean, cut to the chase? I *am* concerned about her health, her physical health and...and her mental health." She swallowed, still finding it painful to think of Ruth's mental capacities diminishing. That was the news that had touched Kayla the deepest and convinced her to come here, her father's suspicion that Ruth might be entering the first stages of senility. Her grandmother was the sharpest businesswoman Kayla had ever known, a vital part of Brayton's all her married life, even before taking the helm twelve years ago when her husband died.

She also happened to be the closest thing Kayla had ever known to a mother.

She wished she'd come home at Christmas. Gordon claimed that Ruth had been exhibiting some fairly odd behavior even then. Maybe she could have talked to her and averted this dangerous new turn of events. Instead, Kayla had stayed in Chicago because she'd found herself shorthanded at the store due to illness among her staff. In addition, Frank had asked her to spend the holiday season with his family, and since their relationship had progressed to the point where they were discussing marriage, she had agreed.

"Explain." Matt Reed's eyes narrowed. "What exactly do you mean, you're concerned about her mental health?"

Kayla swallowed a mouthful of vegetables. They went down like a lump of sand. "Well, it seems she hasn't been acting herself lately. She's become forgetful and vague. A neighbor passed her on the street recently and she walked right by without even saying hello. Other times, her behavior has just been inappropriate. You know, smiling when nothing is funny?"

"Everyone daydreams, Kayla."

Kayla felt a tremor in her stomach. That was exactly what she'd said to Gordon yesterday.

"Yes, but did you ever catch my grandmother at it?" she said, Gordon's reply slipping automatically from her lips.

Matt Reed's frown turned dark.

"One day Gordon stopped by her house and a Salvation Army truck was hauling away most of her wardrobe. Another time he got there right after she'd returned from the beauty salon." She paused, lost in remembered dismay.

"What did she have done?"

"Had her hair cut and permed." Kayla tried to envision her tall, aristocratic grandmother with a short, permed style. And failed. Ruth's elegant, satin-smooth chignon had been her hallmark for as long as Kayla could remember.

"Two weeks later she had it dyed," she added somberly. "Blond." The ache in her heart sharpened.

"Kayla, it isn't unusual for a person to perm and dye her hair."

"I know. But it's totally uncharacteristic for Ruth Brayton. And her wardrobe? My grandmother always bought classic, timeless clothing of only the finest quality, clothing that needed no replacing because of changing styles.

"What really disturbed us, though," she went on, now quoting her father, "was discovering that she had been stepping out with your father. Dating, for heaven's sake!"

The fork Matt was lifting stopped halfway to his mouth. Slowly he lowered it. "And what's wrong with two elderly people going out to dinner once in a while?"

Kayla realized too late she'd backed herself into a corner.

Matt's gray eyes went cold and forbidding. "What you're afraid of is that your grandmother, with her diminished capacities, is being taken advantage of. Right? And who more capable of doing such a thing than the man who knows her finances inside out?"

"N-not exactly. I..."

"Don't quibble, Kayla. I've already heard it from your father and brother. You're afraid my father is defrauding Ruth somehow, sweet-talking her into paying for this vacation they're taking, or maybe he's dipping into her blue chip stocks or her savings."

Kayla kept her eyes lowered. No, she thought. What really scared her father and brother—and now her, as well—was that Philip Reed was plotting to take over Brayton's. They feared he intended to marry Ruth and outlive her. He was a significantly younger man, her father said. Considering Ruth's health, Philip was probably banking on that happening real soon, too.

Then, as her widower, he'd inherit her position as chairman of the board of Brayton's, which, the way their corporation was set up, practically translated into *ownership* of Brayton's.

With enough finesse, Philip might inherit the rest of Ruth's assets, too, depending on how many legal documents he could coerce her to change—her big old mausoleum of a house in Newton, which Kayla loved, her priceless antiques and paintings, her insurance policies and bond funds and savings...

The thought of these assets leaving the family terrified Lloyd, but not half so much as the thought of losing control of Brayton's, having an outsider take over. As he'd said yesterday, it wasn't as if there had ever been a question as to who would succeed his mother when she retired. He had been running the factory since he was in his twenties.

As Gordon was now, Kayla thought, fighting a small wave of despondency.

She didn't voice any of these fears, however, just on the chance that they hadn't occurred to Matt Reed or his father—although she didn't think that chance was likely.

"All right," Kayla conceded, "I admit it. I am concerned about her finances, but only insofar as they're tied to the problem of her health. The two come as a package. Please, can't you see our side? We love her and are worried sick about her. Why won't you help?"

Matt shook his head, laughing caustically. "You people are incredible. You think I should *help* you? After you accuse my father of plotting to swindle one of his lifelong friends and clients? After you accuse me of being in collusion? How can you not see that as a monumental insult? For that alone I should toss you out, never mind for the damage you could do to my reputation if word of these accusations spreads." He seemed truly angry, not only at her father and Gordon, but at her, as well.

But then, what better way to obfuscate an issue if you were guilty?

"I'm sorry. It wasn't meant as an insult. But if you put yourself in our position, I think you'll understand our concern."

"Oh, I understand it, all right. You Braytons have gone paranoid about your money."

It wasn't just money, she wanted to shout. It was Brayton's, a company her great-great-grandfather had struggled to establish in the 1800s; it was the factory, warm and busy, smelling of wood and varnish and noisy with machinery; it was specialized knowledge of clock movements, appreciation of design, a century-long heritage of quality and pride.

And it was Kayla's retail stores!

"How do you explain their dating, then? They've known each other for thirty-five years. Are we supposed to believe your father is suddenly smitten with Gran now? Uh-uh. The timing is just too convenient. Furthermore, what about the furtiveness of your father's actions? If his intentions are so honorable, why did they run off without telling anyone, hm? No, I'm afraid my grandmother is being led down a primrose path, deliberately and with malicious intent and—"

"Ms. Brayton," Matt interrupted icily, "has it never occurred to you that the person being taken advantage of might not be your grandmother?"

Kayla went still, momentarily confused. When his meaning came clear, she reared back. "That's absurd!"

"Why? Because he isn't quite as wealthy as Ruth?" The cold winter light pouring in the windows accentuated the hardness of his face. "He has money, more than you Braytons are apparently aware of."

"But Ruth would never..." Her voice thinned. She shook her head and repeated, "It's absurd."

Matt Reed sighed heavily and looked off into space. "There are all sorts of ways to be taken advantage of, Kayla, and sometimes financially is the least of them." He pushed aside his plate, his meal only half eaten.

Kayla watched him for several puzzling seconds. "I don't have a clue what you're talking about, but if you think my grandmother is taking advantage of your father, why did you help them run off?"

"Because I like Ruth, dammit, and she needed..." He paused abruptly, letting the thought trail off. He thrust a hand through his hair, angry, frustrated. Kayla wondered if he realized he'd just admitted that he had indeed participated in the getaway, something that had been just a supposition until now.

She frowned at him across the table. Yesterday, talking with her father and Gordon, she'd expressed doubt regarding Matt's involvement with his father's alleged scheme. But, as her father had explained, if Philip succeeded in marrying Ruth and inherited her estate at her death, that inheritance would eventually end up with Matt, who'd inherit it from his father. Perhaps Lloyd was right, after all; Matt really had contrived the plot with his father. Kayla wasn't sure why that thought bothered her so much. Had she been hoping for better from him?

"Will you please share the phone number with me?" she tried once again.

"No," he shot back.

"Why not?"

"Because I don't want to."

She couldn't help laughing. "You don't want to." She picked up her purse and rose. "Fine. Have it your way. Sorry to have taken up so much of your time, Mr. Reed. I'll see myself to the door."

As she walked away, she heard him scrape back his chair. She had her hand on the doorknob when he said, "Wait. Hold it."

She paused, suppressing a tiny smile of satisfaction. Her father and Gordon had urged her to try Matt Reed first. He was the quickest route to finding Ruth, and if marriage was indeed Philip's intent, they were racing the clock.

But if Matt didn't cooperate, she needn't fawn. To hell with him, Lloyd had said. They'd find her grandmother anyway.

She turned to find Matt scowling.

"What've you got up your sleeve?"

"Pardon me?"

"You wouldn't be ending this discussion so soon if you didn't have an alternate plan."

"Can't get anything by you, by golly," she mocked.

"Is your father planning to go ahead with his threats of pressing criminal charges?"

Her stomach dropped to somewhere around her knees.

In her continued silence, he clarified, "You know, for my role in aiding and abetting a kidnapping?"

"No, um, no." Her father had threatened *that?* "But you're right about the alternate plan. I came here hoping to get your cooperation, but we'll find my grandmother anyway. You see, we've already contacted a private investigator who says it shouldn't take more than a few days to locate her."

Matt Reed's jaw looked as hard as the granite that dominated the decor of his office. "I see. And when he does, are you planning to have this private eye bind and gag her and throw her on a plane back to Boston? Do you think my father has brainwashed her or is holding her against her will?"

"No, the investigator's job is merely to locate her. As I said, *I* want to visit her. And I will, make no mistake about it."

He eyed her speculatively. "What would you say if I told you the PI will be wasting his time? She's unfindable."

She eyed him just as speculatively. Was he telling the truth or calling her bluff? "I'd say, get yourself a good lawyer, Mr. Reed, because if any harm comes to her—financial, physical, emotional or otherwise—be prepared to suffer the consequences."

The shrill ring of a phone made them both jump. Kayla glanced toward Matt's desk, at the phone and console of intercom buttons, but strangely the ring wasn't coming from that direction. Then she noticed Matt's eyes fixed on a different phone, one resting on a table beside a reading chair. His breathing had gone curiously shallow.

The phone rang again. And a third time. Obviously, it wasn't part of the office system, and if Matt didn't answer it, no one was going to. His eyes darted to Kayla, darted back to the phone.

Finally the answering machine clicked on, his deep resonant voice instructing, "Leave a message. I'll get back as soon as possible."

Kayla felt uncomfortable eavesdropping on what was apparently a private line. Uncomfortable, that is, until she heard a similarly deep voice say, "Matthew? It's Dad," and then her grandmother adding, "And Ruth."

One breathless gasp was all Kayla allowed herself before dashing to the phone.

CHAPTER TWO

AS FAST as Kayla was, Matt was even faster. "Yes, hello, I'm here," he said in a rush.

Kayla gripped his arm and tried to tug the phone away. "I want to speak to my grandmother."

Turning aside, Matt covered his exposed ear. "What? No, that wasn't anything. Go on, you were saying?"

"It was *too* something," she hollered. "Gran, this is Kayla."

"Hold on, Dad." Matt pressed the phone to his lapel. "Will you shut up!"

"I want to speak to my grandmother, and if you don't let me, I'll raise such a ruckus you won't be able to hear a single word."

His scowl blackened. "Have you ever been thrown out of a building, Ms. Brayton?"

"Can't say that I have. Why don't you go call security?"

He growled before replacing the phone to his ear. "Dad? I've got a little problem. Kayla Brayton is here and... Oh, hello, Mrs. Brayton." He grimaced. "Yes, you heard right." He paused again, listening, then with simmering resignation, handed over the phone.

"Gran?"

"Kayla?"

At the sound of her grandmother's voice, Kayla's eyes grew hot with impending tears.

"Kayla, what a marvelous surprise!"

"Gran, are you all right?"

"Of course I'm all right. How are you?"

Kayla swallowed repeatedly, but the lump in her throat refused to dissolve. "I'm fine, Gran. Well, worried actually. You took off so abruptly and... Where *are* you?"

Matt's look grew thunderous. He plugged another phone into a nearby outlet, and the next moment he'd cut in on the conversation.

"Mrs. Brayton?"

"Oh, are you both on the line?"

"Yes," he replied, giving Kayla another look of caution.

"How nice." Aside Ruth called, "Phil, pick up the other phone, then we can all talk at once."

He did, and for a while it seemed they all did talk at once, asking how everyone was and what the weather was like.

But eventually small talk subsided and Ruth asked, "What ever are you two doing together? I have to say I'm thoroughly confused. Delighted—but confused."

Matt forced a laugh past the implications in the word "delighted." "Kayla is here because... because we recently discovered there's something we'd both like to do very much, and we were just discussing the possibility of combining efforts."

"Really? And what is this intriguing thing you'd both like to do?"

Yes, what? Kayla demanded with her eyes.

"We'd both like to fly down to visit you."

Kayla responded as if she'd been bonked on the forehead with a two-by-four. Her mouth dropped open in protest, but Matt immediately placed his fingers over her parted lips. The unexpected touch stunned her into speechlessness.

From the other end of the line came a flurry of muffled whispers.

Then, "We weren't exactly counting on visitors, Matthew," Philip Reed said apologetically. "We're here on vacation."

"I realize that, and we wouldn't dream of intruding. It goes without saying we'd stay at a hotel."

More whispers. Kayla took the opportunity to cover her mouthpiece and in a frantic whisper demand, "What the hell are you doing, Reed?"

He covered his phone, too, and rasped back, "If you go, I go, no two ways about it. Is that clear?"

Kayla blinked, then fought a triumphant grin. Apparently her grandmother was eminently findable, and Matt knew he'd been bested.

"Kayla, are you there?"

"Yes, Gran."

"You know I love you, dear, and I'd agree to almost anything you asked..."

"Mrs. Brayton," Matt interrupted, "the plain truth is, your son has hired a private investigator to track you down."

Kayla gaped at him. How dared he drop her ace without her permission.

"Oh, dear, oh, dear," Ruth lamented. Philip muttered, "I figured something like this would happen."

"But there's an alternative," Matt offered. "That's for us to visit, Kayla and I. If we do and Kayla is able to come back with a report that you're okay, Mrs. Brayton, that might appease your son and you can continue your vacation without further harassment."

"You and Kayla together?" Ruth asked dubiously.

"Yes," Matt answered.

He and Kayla waited through another spate of whispers.

"You had no right to say anything about the private eye," she lashed out.

"All's fair, kid."

She made a face at him. He made one back.

"Matthew?"

"Yes, Dad."

"You'll still keep our whereabouts a secret?"

"Of course. Kayla won't know where we're going until we get there."

If looks could kill, she hoped Matt got her message.

"All right, son, you can come."

Kayla was so astonished she momentarily forgot her anger, grabbed Matt's sleeve and gave it a few uninhibited yanks.

"In fact, now that we've discussed it," Ruth Brayton added, "we're really looking forward to your visit. But you'll have to make it soon."

"How soon, Gran?"

"Sunday, Monday the latest."

Kayla gulped. "I'm not sure I—"

Matt cut her off. "No problem. I'll call back after I've made flight arrangements so you'll know when to expect us."

"Great," his father said. "Oh, and don't worry about a hotel. We have lots of room here."

As soon as they'd hung up, Kayla turned to Matt, fists planted on her hips. "Thanks a million."

"You're welcome. For what?"

"I have obligations, you know. *You* might be able to drop everything at a whim, but I—"

"Drop everything at a whim! Lady, look around!" He made a strangled sound deep in his throat. "Besides, I thought seeing your grandmother was of the utmost urgency."

She bared her teeth in a frustrated snarl. "I'll have to call my office and rearrange my whole—"

Matt was already holding out a phone to her. Never one to back down from a dare, Kayla snatched it from him. She realized her complaints were absurd. She'd reached her objective, after all; she'd got herself invited to Ruth and Philip's hideaway in the Bahamas. She just hadn't expected Matt Reed to be a part of the deal.

With Matt using the office line to call his travel agent, Kayla made the call to the store in Chicago using his private line. Frank answered on the fifth ring.

She could tell he was busy and didn't fully understand what she was doing, but at the moment she didn't feel up to explaining. She did promise to call him later, at his apartment, when there would be more time to talk.

Luckily she always traveled with an electronic calendar, and while Matt studied the airline listings scrolling up his computer screen, Kayla and Frank shuffled appointments and reassigned tasks. She and Matt hung up at almost the same time.

"Well?" Matt's left eyebrow had a way of quirking whenever he asked a question.

"I cleared my week."

"That's fortunate since we have a confirmed flight."

Kayla went to the conference table, poured another glass of water and swallowed a couple of aspirins she'd dug from her purse. "When?"

"Sunday, eleven o'clock. I'll meet you at the American Airlines ticket counter around ten, ten-fifteen."

"And when are we returning?"

"I've left that open-ended, but it shouldn't be more than a few days. Oh, and you'll need your passport."

"I don't have a passport."

"Proof of voter registration, then. Bahama immigration accepts that in place of a passport. You'd better call City Hall in Chicago and have them mail it overnight."

"I can do better than that. I'll go to City Hall in person. I'm still registered here, in Boston."

"Oh. How come?"

She shrugged, avoiding his gaze. "I've moved so many times the past few years, it just seemed easier. I vote by absentee ballot." She carefully set the glass down. "Well, then, I guess it's settled."

"Yes."

The intercom on his desk buzzed. "Mr. Reed, your one o'clock is here."

"Thanks, Sara. I'll just be a minute."

Was it really only one o'clock? Kayla was used to moving in the fast lane—but this was mad!

"Well, I guess I'll s-see you at Logan," she stammered.

He looked up, distracted, his mind already on his next appointment. "Yes."

Kayla nodded goodbye and on legs that wobbled walked out of the office. Good Lord, she thought, she'd left snowy Chicago only yesterday thinking she'd be returning by Sunday night. Instead, she'd be somewhere in the sunny Bahamas trying not to notice that Matt Reed, the love of her life for too many painful teenage years, just happened to be along, as well.

Lloyd Brayton pulled to the busy curb at the appropriate airline terminal but didn't turn off the engine. "You'll call me, won't you?" he said, his words more a statement than a request.

Kayla stared out the Lincoln's windshield, gritty with road salt, and shivered even though the car was comfortably heated. The temperature had plummeted the previous night, freezing the sleety rain that had fallen earlier so that everything was coated in ice this morning, even the old dirty snow piled on the sides of Logan's roadways.

"I'll try, Dad. I'll do my best. But if for some reason I don't get the chance, please don't worry."

"How can I not worry with Matt Reed along to cause trouble?" His fingers tightened around the steering wheel.

She'd told her father the results of her meeting with Matt, thinking he'd be pleased. Not only had she managed to talk with Matt, a feat in itself, considering the damage he and Gordon had already done by losing their tempers, but she'd landed the visit with her grandmother, too. So far, however, Lloyd had exhibited nothing but displeasure.

"I know you don't like the idea of Matt going along. Neither do I. But I had no choice. And anyway, I think we may have more in common with him than we realized. As I told you, he didn't seem all that happy about his father's being in the Bahamas with Gran, either."

Her father cast her a withering glance, making her realize she'd said the wrong thing yet again.

"I don't buy that, and neither should you. He's a smooth operator, Kayla. He hasn't gotten where he is today by being anyone's fool, and I haven't a doubt he and his father are in on this together. Be careful, young lady."

She wilted under his reproof.

"It makes no sense that he'd be concerned about his father," Lloyd continued. "Your grandmother has all the money she needs. She certainly doesn't need Philip's. I'm sure Matt is going along on this trip merely to keep you from getting close to her and bringing her home."

Kayla pressed her lips tight. That thought had crossed her mind, too.

"And you will bring her back, correct?"

She swallowed. "Correct."

"Good. So, I'll expect you—when?"

"I'm hoping Wednesday. I've got to fly out to San Francisco again early next week."

"Fine. Three days. That should be sufficient to talk some sense into your grandmother," he said, glossing over her reference to the new store. "Well, I'd better let you off."

"Mm. Cars are backing up behind you."

"Oh, are they?" He glanced in the rearview mirror. "I was referring to brunch with Gordon."

"Oh. Oh, I'm sorry. I didn't realize..."

"No big deal. We go to brunch almost every Sunday."

Somehow the comment didn't make her feel any better. It only underscored the fact that she was drifting farther from this man, while his relationship with his son was deepening.

She got out of the car, hunching against the frigid wind, opened the back door and, after hauling out her briefcase and garment bag, set them on the sidewalk.

"Well, okay," she said, bending to look into the car where her father still sat, hands on the wheel.

"Remember, don't let Reed come between you and your grandmother."

"I won't."

"And bring her home safely, you hear? Brayton Clocks, too."

"I will."

"I hope so. We're depending on you, Kayla."

Against all her efforts, her throat was closing up on her. She watched him reach for the stick shift, felt her dejection like an icy hand squeezing her heart and abruptly called out, "Dad, wait."

The Lincoln took a little lurch. Kayla ran around to the driver's side and opened the door.

"What is it, Kayla?" Her father looked genuinely puzzled.

A nervous tremor racked her. She hesitated, biting her lip. "I ... I just wanted to say bye." Before her courage deserted her, she leaned in and gave him a quick, tight hug.

"Oh," he said, giving her encircling arm an uncertain pat.

She felt the stiffness in his shoulders and backed away. His expression was uneasy. "See ya, Dad." Without waiting for a response she hurried to her luggage and fled through the glass doors of the terminal.

She spotted Matt standing by the airline ticket counter, right where they'd agreed to meet two days ago. For a moment she halted, her mood shifting quickly from melancholy to... to something else, which she preferred not to examine. My Lord, he really was a stunning specimen. Her imagination hadn't been playing tricks on her Friday in his office.

He was dressed in a dark gray topcoat, open, a black cableknit sweater, crisp white shirt and neatly creased trousers. Like her, he was toting a garment bag and a briefcase.

As she resumed walking down the concourse toward him, she felt his gaze moving over her, from her neat French twist to the Hermés scarf tied artfully around the collar of her black wool coat, down to her high-heeled black leather boots.

In that instant she realized that no two people had ever looked less like a couple heading to the tropics than they did. But then, it *was* eighteen degrees here in Boston. And they *did* look rather smart.

"Hi," she said, smiling guardedly.

He nodded without expression. "Is that all you're taking?" His cool, crisp tone brought her crashing back to the fact that they were hardly on amicable terms and she was a fool for noticing he was any sort of specimen other than one carrying a great deal of hostility toward her and her family.

"Yes, this is all."

"Good. Carryons make getting in and out of airports so much faster."

"Yes, I know," she said, tight-lipped.

"Fine. Come on, then. Let's get our boarding passes."

They joined one of several long, slow-moving lines. They kept their eyes fixed forward and said nothing.

Kayla still couldn't believe she was doing this. It was the most bizarre arrangement she'd ever been involved in. She hardly knew Matt Reed. Except for that meeting at his office—and one highly forgettable date eons ago— he was a stranger to her, a stranger who just might be conspiring against her and her family. Yet she was traveling with him.

Where she was traveling she still had no idea—which added another dimension to the bizarre nature of this venture.

The line moved very slowly, and the silence between them began to throb. Matt shifted his weight, coughed and finally said, "I guess I can tell you now, we're flying to Orlando. We have a connecting flight there."

"Oh." Kayla scanned the crowd around them, noting the large number of families filling the lines. "DisneyWorld," she said.

"Yes. I believe this is school vacation week."

Kayla wondered at this foray into polite conversation. "It's been a terrible winter, too," she added.

"Yes." Matt pushed his briefcase ahead with his foot. Another length of silence followed. Kayla cleared her throat. He glanced at her from the corner of his eye.

"Ever been to the Bahamas before?"

"No," she answered.

"Where'd your family go on vacations when you were young?"

"We didn't. My family isn't big on vacation. You?"

"Been to the Bahamas? No. We didn't go many places, either, and now—" he shrugged "—I don't have much time."

"I know what you mean." She loosened her scarf and unbuttoned her coat, revealing the navy suit and white blouse she'd worn to his office.

"You did bring other clothes, I hope."

She cast him a dry look. "I went shopping yesterday." A sudden memory flashed through her mind of the colorful summer outfits she'd seen, blooming like hothouse flowers in Filene's vacation-wear department. She'd easily resisted them, though, buying instead one serviceable pair of tan chino shorts, a green wraparound skirt, two polo shirts—one tan, one white—and a pair of white flats.

"I didn't go overboard, though. I resent buying clothes I don't need."

"I understand. We shouldn't be gone long, anyway." Matt nudged his briefcase forward another few inches. She did the same.

What am I doing here? she wondered again, feeling the absurdity of the situation on a fresh wave of anxiety. She should be in Chicago right now, driving to the store to prepare for Sunday business.

"Come on," Matt said. "We're next."

For a while, the process of procuring boarding passes, going through security and finding the right gate kept them both on the move, but once they'd found seats in the waiting area, Kayla began to feel edgy again. The rumble of jets taking off was lending the trip a reality she hadn't fully felt until then. But what really made her nervous was the announcement that their flight was being delayed a half-hour so the plane could be deiced.

Luckily she'd brought along enough work to keep her busy during the tense wait. She opened her briefcase, carefully lifted out a laptop computer, and booted up the inventory file for the store in Baltimore. Matt opened his briefcase, too, an ingeniously compartmentalized item that housed a laptop, a fax machine and a cellular phone, and while she pored over her figures, he concentrated on numbers of his own.

Minutes spun out. Kayla read the columns on her miniature screen—and read them again, realizing she was absorbing nothing. Beside her Matt shifted his weight, quietly cleared his throat and tapped his fingers on his thigh.

She tried to look at him without turning her head. All she managed to see was his left leg, ankle crossed over the opposite knee, charcoal flannel stretched taut along the muscular thigh.

She could also see his left arm. He'd removed his coat and pushed up the sleeves of his black sweater, revealing forearms that seemed more suited to a bricklayer than a desk jockey. At his wrist ticked an elaborate watch, which, among other functions, provided the time of day in three world capitals. His hand was broad and capable-looking, with clean, blunt-filed nails and just a feathering of dark hair over the knuckles. She'd never paid much attention to a man's hands before and was dismayed to find that his fascinated her. Cautiously she turned and lifted her gaze to his face.

He wasn't reading, either. His deep gray eyes were fixed on the runways. A pensive look clouded his expression. Inadvertently her gaze moved to his mouth. She'd kissed that mouth, felt its texture and warmth against her own. And she thought, how very bizarre that two people could share such an intimate act and then sit in an airport ten years later pretending to be strangers.

Not that she was disappointed they'd chosen to take that route. Actually, she was relieved. Brief and meaningless as the incident had been, it still caused her enough embarrassment to make just being with him a painfully

self-conscious experience. She certainly didn't want to
talk about it.

Kayla fixed her gaze on a jet being refueled. Gradually
her vision blurred and her thoughts turned inward.

She'd been in her third year at Briarwood, a private
all-girls academy that her father had persuaded her to
attend after a somewhat normal childhood in public
school. She never felt she fit in at Briarwood. Not that
it was really all that exclusive—most of its students were
local—and even if it had been, her family certainly had
the credentials to pass muster. Nevertheless, too many
of the girls who attended the academy had a falsely inflated idea of their station in the world.

Cliques abounded, painful delineations between who
was in and who was out. Part of the problem resided in
the fact that Briarwood included a grammar school, and
the girls who'd attended it had formed their alliances
years before reaching the upper grades.

But being a latecomer wasn't Kayla's only problem.
She was also an oddity. With her grandmother having
stepped into the void created when Kayla's mother died,
Kayla's clothing and general appearance had always reflected a mature, almost stodgy view of what was in style.
Not until she attended Briarwood, however, did Kayla
feel the bite of open criticism.

Looking back, she suspected that even the most stylish
clothing wouldn't have helped. She'd never considered
herself pretty. She was too plain, too ordinary. But at
sixteen she'd been downright pitiful.

She'd already reached her adult height of five feet six,
but her weight had not caught up, remaining under one
hundred pounds. She had no curves worth mentioning,
wore no makeup, and her shoulder-length blond hair
hung limp and scorched from a home permanent she'd
foolishly given herself when Ruth wasn't looking. But
the worst memory of all in Kayla's mental attic of horrors

was her braces, those thick silver bars that gleamed like
the grille of a '57 Buick whenever she opened her mouth.

She'd pleaded with her grandmother not to phone Mr.
Reed, but Ruth hadn't listened. Ruth knew Briarwood's
Christmas dance, held every year at a neighboring
country club, was the highlight of the school's social calendar. She also knew Kayla didn't have any male friends
she felt comfortable inviting as her escort. She said
Philip's son probably had nothing to do the night of the
dance, being home from college on Christmas break,
and would enjoy the chance to go out.

Nothing to do? Matt Reed? Everybody in a twenty-
mile radius knew that Matt Reed had only to pull into
his driveway at the end of a semester and the telephone
would be ringing off the hook. Not that Kayla or anyone
else at Briarwood knew exactly what went on in his life.
They were a little too young to spin in his orbit. But
he'd grown up in the same Boston suburb, attended the
local high school, was a track star and a scholar and an
unabashed hunk. People *knew* Matt Reed. He was one
of those rare individuals who is watched by total
strangers, talked about and legendized.

When her grandmother told her Matt was willing to
escort her to the dance, Kayla's first reaction was astonishment. But within minutes she'd wanted to die, just
crawl under her bed with the dust bunnies and die. He
was too old for her, too popular, too everything.
Everyone was sure to know it was a fix up.

And then the real agony set in. Why on earth had he
accepted? He barely knew her. They'd met a few times
when she'd gone with Ruth to Philip's office and Matt
happened to be there working after school, but he'd
hardly said two sentences to her. Was it because Gran
was Mr. Reed's most important client? Had Matt been
pressured into acquiescing?

The date turned out every bit as torturous as she'd expected. He showed up at her door looking good enough to serve as dessert. She'd just vomited for the second time that evening. In his car, he conversed easily. She developed a stammer. At the country club, he kept the dance steps simple while she still managed to step on his feet.

In spite of everything, he remained a polite and attentive escort. Still, she sensed a restlessness in him, a subtle longing for the night to be over. Unobtrusive glances at his watch. A fidgety tapping of his fingers on the table when conversation stalled.

She suggested they leave before the dance was over, an idea he didn't object to. They left the ballroom located on the upper level, descended the elegant stairway and went round to the cloakroom at the rear of the main foyer. So close to leaving and being able to remember the night as merely uncomfortable...

They both heard the laughter from the adjacent lounge at the same time. They also heard the comments made by people who didn't realize she and Matt were there. Kayla recognized one of the voices as belonging to the leader of the most popular clique in her class. Humiliation flooded her, because the object of the group's amusement was Kayla Brayton.

They were saying just what she'd feared they'd say, that her grandmother had arranged the date. And then someone added she hoped poor Matt wouldn't try to kiss her. Laughter obscured the rest, but Kayla did manage to hear the words "shredded tongue."

She made a blind grab at what she hoped was her coat, but Matt's fingers swiftly closed over her wrist.

"I've changed my mind." A hard edge had entered his voice. "I suddenly have the urge to dance a few more numbers." Before she could protest, he hauled her back up the stairs.

They danced. Oh, how they danced! To the present day, Kayla had experienced nothing quite like it again. At first, she'd been rigid with shock, but it didn't take long for Matt to work his magic. Holding her close, swaying to the slow music, he was the very stuff of her teenage dreams. She was too bright not to realize he was only pretending, but she was also too inexperienced to keep from being affected.

They danced two numbers. After each, he continued to hold her to him, his hands loosely clasped behind her back, while they talked quietly amidst the other couples who'd remained on the dance floor, too, awaiting the next number.

Just as the third song started, Kayla noticed the group from the lounge enter the ballroom. Her pulse quickened, and tension stiffened her shoulders.

"Relax, sweetheart," Matt whispered against her hair. "You're doing fine." His warm breath sent a pleasurable shiver down her back. Still, she couldn't relax. He put a little distance between them and tipped her chin so that she had to look up—into his smoky gray eyes, into his reassuring smile. She couldn't help smiling back. She was still smiling when he lowered his head and kissed her. Braces and all, he kissed her and went on kissing her until her knees turned to water and her heart almost banged its way right through her ribs.

Finally he pulled away and slowly opened his eyes. Kayla opened hers at about the same time, sighing dreamily. "Now we can leave," he whispered.

Neither of them looked toward the small group from the lounge, but Kayla knew they'd been watching. Silence had fallen over every last one.

Matt had driven her halfway home before they spoke. "Are you all right?" he asked quietly, eyes fixed on the road.

"Yes. Yes, of course." She swallowed over the lie. She was not all right. She was still wrapped in a haze of heat and stardust from his kiss, but she would die before she let him know that. "I was fully aware of what you were doing."

He drove on in pensive silence. "Well, I just wanted the matter to be absolutely clear. I...I have a girlfriend back at college. We're pretty serious."

Her throat was tightening. What a pathetic creature she was. Had she actually begun to think he might've felt something for her while they'd been dancing? That the heat building inside her had been a shared reaction?

"I understand. Perfectly. I—" she gulped "—I'm seeing someone, too, but he had to go with his family on a cruise."

"Well, good. I'm relieved you understand." He pulled into the circular driveway in front of her house, switched off the engine and turned to face her. "Kayla, you have a great deal to offer. You're bright, you're funny, you're kind and sincere. And believe it or not, you're going to be a very pretty lady when you grow up. I can tell. So don't let anybody put you down."

With the words "when you grow up" still sending sharp little stabbing pains to her ego, he covered her linked hands with one of his. It was the most brotherly touch she'd ever felt, and it made her utterly wretched.

"Thanks for being my..." My what? she thought. My mercy date? Knight in shining armor? Indentured servant? "Thanks for taking me."

"My pleasure." He'd smiled then, a smile she'd stared at and tried to commit to memory, because even then she'd known she would never see him again.

And she hadn't. Not until two days ago.

"Kayla?"

She jumped at the sound of Matt's voice. She turned her head and gazed at him, lost in transit somewhere between the past and present.

"Where were you?"

Color warmed her cheeks. Had he been talking to her? His eyes were roaming her face, feature by feature. He seemed to be suppressing a smile. Did he still find her young and gauche? Laughable?

She lifted her chin, trying to hide the hurt that stubbornly lingered despite her acquired maturity and outward polish. "Were you saying something?"

"Yes. I asked what you do in Chicago."

She hesitated. "Listen, Matt, before we get on that plane... We both know this isn't a pleasure trip, and quite frankly I'm not much in a mood for conversation. I have work to do and I..."

"I agree. Believe me, I feel just as uncomfortable as you do about our traveling together. We barely know each other, we distrust the hell out of each other, yet for the next five hours we'll practically be joined at the hip. I just thought a little conversation might make the time go faster. I prefer to work, too, but for some reason I can't seem to concentrate, and, well, our flight's just been delayed another twenty minutes."

Kayla shot a glance to the monitor overhead that listed arrivals and departures. Sure enough, their flight wouldn't be taking off until nearly noon. On a surge of frustration compounded by anxiety, she launched herself out of her chair and began to pace.

"Want to get something to eat?" Matt asked, slanting a look at her.

"No." She crossed her arms. "Yes."

They picked up their bags, but when he started walking toward a restaurant, she continued on to a lounge.

"Irish Mist on the rocks, please," she told the bartender.

Matt stared at her, that infuriating left eyebrow cocked. She looked back, daring him to say something.

"Coffee," he said. "Black."

They sat at a small table, quietly sipping their drinks, watching the parade of people moving past. Finally Kayla couldn't take the silence any longer. Matt was right. They had hours to kill—here, on the plane, at the airport in Orlando, on the plane to their mystery destination. It would be unnatural not to talk. Besides, what did she have to be afraid of?

"I...I've been working for Brayton's," she said, dropping the comment so unexpectedly that Matt choked on his coffee.

"Ah, the lady speaks."

Immediately she wished she hadn't.

"I'm sorry. Go on. You work for Brayton's. Retail stores, right?"

She sipped her Irish Mist, studying him under her long lashes. With such a vested interest in Brayton's, he undoubtedly knew every last detail about the company already. He probably even had access to Brayton's financial reports, since his father did their books.

"Yes," she finally answered. "Retail stores."

"Hmm. You were always interested in sales, but as I recall, you'd hoped to work from the factory."

The keenness of his memory unnerved her. "Yes, well, things change," she said evasively. "When I started working full time, after college, I convinced my father to let me open a factory outlet. He was so pleased with the results, I decided to go on the road with my act. We now have retail stores in five major cities. But surely I'm not telling you anything new."

A smile gradually eased its way over his face, crinkling delightful little fan lines outward from his eyes. "You're right. Ruth has mentioned you a few times."

"She has? When?"

"During visits to my office. She's one of my clients."

"One of your...?" Her voice thinned in puzzlement.

"Mm. Gutsy lady. Loves playing with high-risk, high-yield commodities. Says it gives her a rush." He shook his head, smiling.

"My grandmother plays the stock market?"

"Sure. Didn't you know?"

"I knew she had a modest portfolio of blue chip stocks."

"Still does. She hasn't dumped any of her IBM." He tilted his head, studying her expression. "Don't worry. This passion of hers is a recent development, and I've been careful to steer her toward safe investments."

So, Matt handled Ruth's portfolio and knew exactly what she was worth in stocks and bonds. Even while the hair on Kayla's neck was still rising, he said, "Ruth mentioned your stores, but just briefly. I don't know that much about them, and, to be frank, I'm still surprised. For more than a century, Brayton's merely manufactured clocks and sold them wholesale through a catalogue and a team of traveling salesmen."

"We did. Still do. But now there are also my retail stores."

"Interesting." He sipped his coffee. "Are you happy doing what you're doing?"

"Yes, of course." She linked her fingers around her glass and stared at its dark amber contents.

"How does he fit in?"

"He, who?"

"The guy who gave you that ring."

Kayla's gaze shifted to the tiny sapphire on her right hand. "How did you know it was a guy?"

"Just a hunch."

"His name's Frank Schaeffer. He used to be one of our midwest salesmen, but now, well, he's more or less my personal assistant. Partner, really."

"Partner, huh? How long've you known him?"

"Oh, since he started working for Brayton's seven years ago. But we've only dated for the past two."

"Only? I consider that a fairly long time."

"Maybe. But it's better to be safe than sorry."

"Amen to that." He toasted her with his coffee mug. "Do you hear any wedding bells in the near future?"

She shrugged. "We're thinking maybe in another year."

The energy in his eyes seemed to compress. "No kidding?"

"Yes," she bit out. Had he thought she was incapable of attracting anyone with serious intentions?

"And will you continue to work after you're married?"

"Of course. Frank and I will be opening a new store in San Francisco next fall, and we have plans for another in Phoenix the year after."

"All that moving around will be hard on children, if they happen to come along."

"I know. That's why I don't plan to have any for at least ten years. After getting the store in Phoenix on its feet, we'll be moving on to Texas, and then maybe Florida."

Matt's face had become a tight, unreadable mask. "Do you ever plan to settle?"

"Sure. In Chicago." *If* she and Frank got married, she thought, which was still up in the air. But pretending that the matter was settled was somehow proving a balm to her hurt pride. "Chicago is so central, you know, and Frank's family lives there, too. Our target date is seven years from now. That'll give us time to find a house and get ourselves established before we have children."

Matt had pushed away from the table and was eyeing her dubiously, arms folded across his broad chest. "Does your father like him...what's his name, Frank?"

"Yes. Very much. He's the one who...suggested we work together." She'd almost said "fixed us up." "How about you, Matt? What's been happening in your life?"

If he noticed her attempt to change the focus of conversation, he didn't reveal it. "After college I went to work with my father, too. He'd always been just an accountant. I broadened the services he could provide. To make a long story short, business grew, we moved offices and business grew even more. Unfortunately my father retired a few years ago. I have twenty-two employees, but none can hold a candle to him."

"He's retired?"

"Mm." Apparently she looked puzzled because he explained, "He comes in occasionally, to do special accounts like your grandmother's."

"Ah." She focused her gaze on a young couple kissing, saying goodbye. "So, what else has been happening in your life? Last thing I remember, you were madly in love with somebody you went to college with. Whatever happened to her?"

She'd meant the remark as a mild dig. Recalling how popular he'd always been—and apparently still was, if *The Bostonian* could be believed—she fully expected him to have forgotten the girl entirely by now. Therefore she was deeply puzzled when he reached across the table for her glass and downed the remaining contents in one swallow. And she was more than thunderstruck when he grimaced and said, "I married her."

CHAPTER THREE

Just then the announcement went out over the PA system that their flight was boarding. Kayla was so dazed she barely heard it.

"You married her?"

His jaw hardened. "Yes."

"But—" Confusion short-circuited her thoughts.

"We're divorced, Kayla." He stood up so abruptly his chair rocked on two legs. "Come on, it's time to fly."

She followed him through the crowd and onto the plane, burning to ask him what had happened to his marriage, but it was obvious he didn't want to talk about it. Besides, she thought she already knew. Matt Reed simply wasn't the marrying type. In his profile in *The Bostonian* he'd been quoted as saying he enjoyed playing the field and was, in fact, avidly avoiding serious involvement.

"Sorry I wasn't able to get first-class seats," he said, stuffing his garment bag into the compartment overhead. He seemed preoccupied, and despite his set expression, a frown creased his brow. Kayla wondered if mentioning his marriage had unsettled him more than he cared to admit.

She lifted her own bag. "Arrangements were made last minute. I'm amazed you were able to get two seats together." Quarters were tight, and with everyone trying to get settled, she was jostled against him. "Sorry."

He took her bag from her and fit it in with his. "Want to put your coat up there, too?"

44

"Yes, please." She gritted her teeth and subjected herself to several more disconcerting brushes with that solid chest. She knew it meant nothing—her nerves were simply overwrought—but every time she and Matt came within an inch of each other, charged vibrations seemed to zing between them.

Finally she wormed her way into her seat. She gripped the armrests, closed her eyes and blew out a long, shaky breath. It irritated her to find Matt watching her when she opened her eyes, that damned eyebrow of his quirked.

"What's the matter?" he inquired.

"Nothing." She buckled her seat belt, adjusted her air vent and fixed her unseeing gaze out the small window. Truth was, she was terrified. She didn't like flying under the best of conditions, and today's weather was far from the best.

They taxied down one runway and another, moving into takeoff position, and with every yard of ice-glistening asphalt they covered, Kayla's fingers squeezed harder on the armrests. She heard the engine's powerful whine, felt the surge of takeoff—and swallowed convulsively. Her brain grew fevered, rendering her prayers wordless, but they were fiercely fervent nonetheless.

Unexpectedly she felt an arm slide over her shoulders. Just as unexpectedly she pressed her face into the warm safety of Matt's sweater. Even as she was doing it, she knew it was a ridiculous thing to do. Yet she couldn't help herself. Her nerves were raw, and he was there. So solidly there.

"It's okay," he murmured, his hand cradling the back of her head. "Planes have been flying out of here all morning. Nothing's happened, not a single mishap. We're fine, we're fine."

And because he said so, she did feel better. Still, they'd reached twenty thousand feet before she was able to sit back. Her skirt had twisted, and as she set it right, tugging it over her knees, self-consciousness overtook her. Beside her Matt chuckled.

"Stop it," she hissed, her cheeks growing hot.

He continued to be amused. "Who would've thought it?"

She wasn't quite sure what he was referring to, her fear of flying or how readily she'd turned to him for comfort.

"It isn't funny, Matthew. We took off in prime accident conditions."

"You're right. You're right." But the laugh lines on his face continued to mock her.

"I have work to do." Brusquely she reached for her briefcase and he followed suit, but the episode had broken through much of the stiffness between them. They worked comfortably and diligently until lunch was served.

It had been a relief to be momentarily distracted. But now that they were eating, elbows bumping as they sliced into their lasagna, Matt became an all-consuming presence again.

They eased into conversation, about airplane food, about their concern they catch their connecting flight. But finally she decided to ask the question that had been preying on her thoughts since they'd boarded. "Matt?"

"Mm."

She hesitated. "What was your wife's name?" She winced. What a cop-out. She didn't give a hoot what the woman's name was.

Matt's eyes went cool. "Candace," he said.

"Pretty." She nodded—stupidly, she thought. "When did you marry her?"

"The summer after we graduated from college."

She nodded again, like one of those dogs in the rear window of a car. "I guess I missed seeing it in the paper."

"The wedding was in Lenox. That's where she was from."

"Ah." Nod, nod. "But you lived in Boston after you were married."

"Yes."

"Because of your work?"

"And hers. She's in advertising."

"Ah." Kayla kept her gaze fixed on the seat ahead of her. "I hope you don't think I'm prying, but I'd really be interested to know...what went wrong. Maybe I can avoid making the same mistake in my own life."

Matt breathed out a quiet laugh of derision. "What happened, my curious friend, was that Candace was into ten-year plans."

Kayla's lips fell open, slack with confusion, until she remembered her own agenda and realized his derision was aimed at her. "Oh." She blinked rapidly, looking at her meal tray.

"Sorry. I didn't mean to put you down." Matt scrubbed at his head, looking frustrated. "Candace was right, of course. She was right about everything, including our separation. We each had so much we wanted to accomplish in our careers. It would've been wrong to tie ourselves to a home and children."

"But you didn't think so then."

"No, at twenty-three I wanted it all, the whole enchilada." He smiled scornfully. "I was *very* young."

"And now?"

He gave her one of his most effective cocked-eyebrow looks. "Not on your life. I enjoy being single, Kayla. I enjoy my freedom, and I intend to continue enjoying it as long as my work remains the center of my life."

Kayla was thankful the flight attendant interrupted to clear their trays. She was beginning to feel terribly uncomfortable. Apparently so was Matt because, as soon as the young women moved on, he said, "Listen, Kayla, all that unpleasantness happened a long time ago. Candace and I were young, our marriage was brief, and, well, I'd just as soon forget it, okay?''

He lifted his briefcase then and immersed himself in his work with a concentration that cut her off as effectively as a solid stone wall.

Which was just as well, she decided, opening her laptop again. Preoccupation with the events of Matt's life was totally inappropriate. She had to focus on her grandmother and reserve her energy for the situation that lay ahead.

But a few minutes later Kayla's forehead was resting on the cool vibrating window and her thoughts were lost somewhere in the clouds. She was beginning to understand why she felt so uncomfortable traveling with Matt, why she'd been reluctant to talk to him at the airport— why she hadn't even wanted to visit his office. It wasn't just that he'd been witness to the most embarrassing moment of her youth. And it wasn't because they were engaged in this present hostility regarding her grandmother.

Instinctively she'd shied away from him for a more personal reason. She'd known he was a confirmed bachelor, someone who was willing to enjoy a woman's company, but who drew a firm line at commitment. Kayla hadn't wanted to be with him because, in short, she'd wanted to protect herself.

And the reason for that . . . was crazy. Surely she'd outgrown the vulnerability of her teenage years. Hadn't she?

But the truth was as plain as the adrenaline that fizzed through her blood whenever she looked at Matt. In spite of the fact that she was involved with another man, in spite of time and all common sense, the vulnerability remained. And if the vulnerability remained, so did the danger of her being hurt again.

And she would be hurt, if she got pulled in. Matt had never thought twice about her as a female. If anything, he'd found her pitiable, and it wasn't likely he'd experience a change of heart in the next few days. Even if he did—and of course he wouldn't; the thought was ridiculous—his aversion to serious involvement would limit whatever relationship might develop to a temporary fling.

But she wouldn't be pulled in, and that solved that. She was a far different person from the girl of ten years ago. She was a mature, disciplined woman, able to control what she did and felt, and during this visit, controlled was exactly what she planned to be. It shouldn't be hard. All she needed to do was stay focused on the fact that she and Matt were enemies. And if that failed, she'd remember Frank, the wonderful man waiting for her in Chicago.

Kayla sighed and closed her eyes. Matt Reed was exhausting her. *Think of Gran,* she reprimanded herself. *Think of the problems that lay ahead.* And she did. With an effort she put Matt from her mind.

She wished she were better prepared for the changes she expected to find in her grandmother. Although she'd had a couple of days to adjust to the word "senility," and although she'd sat down with herself and philosophized about the inevitability of aging, the truth was she *hadn't* adjusted. She loved Ruth so much, how could she?

Kayla heard Matt speaking. To her? She opened her eyes expectantly, but he had the airplane phone to his ear and was engrossed in a discussion with someone named Rob. One of his employees, she assumed from the nature of the conversation. Kayla decided Matt had the right idea. Work. She turned to her laptop and soon was as deeply engrossed as he.

Because their flight had been delayed, they made their connection in Florida with barely enough time to peel off their outer wear, fill out immigration forms and dash outside to their waiting plane. Kayla did manage to learn that their destination was Grand Bahama Island, but she didn't get the chance to call her father and tell him so.

As she hurried across the field toward the plane, she was thankful she'd had the foresight to change out of her boots into her new flat-heeled shoes while still en route from Boston.

"Do you believe this heat?" Matt stuffed his sweater into his garment bag and handed it over to a luggage handler who slid it into the small plane's cargo bin.

"Like passing through a time warp." Kayla lifted her face to the brilliantly shining Florida sun. "After what we left behind, it's hard to believe that any place on earth could be without snow."

"He wants your bag, Kayla."

"Oh." She handed off her luggage and stepped back to view the activity around the loudly humming plane.

"Is the size of this thing going to bother you?"

Kayla grimaced. "It is rather small, isn't it?"

"About a thirty-seater."

"It's odd, with all the flying I've done, I've never had to actually walk out onto a field before. I've always boarded through a skyway." She laughed nervously as Matt took her arm and started toward the stairs where other passengers were boarding. "I feel like I'm caught inside a 1940s movie."

"Mm," Matt agreed. "A war movie. Black and white. *Casablanca,* maybe?"

"Good choice." Kayla smiled at him over her shoulder. "Then I guess it's time for one of us to say, 'This could be the beginning of a beautiful friendship.'" She continued up the stairs.

"Kayla?"

She half-turned, pausing on the top step. "Yes?"

With his eyes locked on hers and a smile working at the edges of his mouth, Matt said, "This could be the beginning of a beautiful friendship."

Something in his expression made her mouth go dry, but before she could sort out what it was, a flight attendant said, "Right this way, miss."

They flew low, at about six thousand feet, low enough to clearly see the changing landscape and then the ocean, the dark blue of the Gulf Stream, the aqua and brilliant turquoise of the shallower waters as they neared Grand Bahama.

Kayla had opened a trade magazine upon boarding, but she gave it only an occasional glance. The myriad small islands and cays they flew over kept drawing her gaze—and touching a sense of delight she hadn't felt since she was a child. So many drifts of sand dotted with palms, so many uninhabited paradises to lose oneself in and play Robinson Crusoe...

She gave her head a snap to shake out the fluff and screwed her attention on the magazine. She wasn't here on vacation, she reminded herself. She was only staying three days, four at the very most, and within that time she had to pull off a very important mission.

Still, when Grand Bahama came into view, her nerve ends were tingling again. How could they not? This world was so different from the one she knew.

The island was long, boomerang shaped, seventy miles in its east to west length, nine miles across at its widest expanse. Most of the population lived within the modern city of Freeport, leaving the rest of the island a wilderness of palmetto and Marco pine. The southern coast of Freeport, the Lucaya Beach region, was a mecca for sun-loving vacationers. From her bird's-eye view, Kayla could see it all, mangrove swamp, forests, industrial areas, golf courses, luxury hotels and beaches along the far coast.

She was so intrigued by their approach, she didn't realize Matt had leaned across the seat to look out the window, too. Not until she felt his breath on her cheek. She cleared her throat and sat back carefully, feigning disinterest in the view. Looking a little chagrined, he did the same.

Freeport International was a much smaller airport than either Kayla or Matt had expected—or the term "international" would imply. Disembarking from the plane, Kayla glanced in surprise from the modest pink stucco terminal to the handful of quiet runways shimmering in the late afternoon heat. Exotic trees and flowers deepened her sense of having entered an alien world.

Immigration and customs officials were used to processing hordes of vacationers each day, and lines moved quickly. But not quickly enough for Kayla, although she didn't realize she was exhibiting impatience until one of the baggage handlers laughed and told her to slow down. "You be on island time now, sugar," he said in the clipped, delightfully musical speech pattern she was quickly coming to associate with native Bahamians.

"Was I impolite?" she asked Matt under her breath as they left the desk.

"Not that I could see. New Englanders just talk faster than most other people. That's all it was."

"Oh, I didn't realize that about us. Hey, can you please take smaller steps? My legs aren't as . . ." The rest of her words got swallowed up when she collided with his left shoulder. Matt hadn't just slowed down; he'd come to a dead stop.

"Oh, Lord!" he muttered.

Kayla tipped her head to study his expression, then followed his gaze. "Oh!" she concurred, just as two elderly people began to make their way forward.

"Kayla, how good to see you." A deeply tanned Ruth Brayton wrapped her wiry arms around her stunned granddaughter and hugged with more strength than Kayla had thought possible. She dropped her bags and hugged Ruth in return. On the fringe of her vision she noticed Matt and his father greeting each other with similar affection.

Kayla stepped back but still held onto Ruth's hands. "Oh, Gran, let me look at you."

A wry twinkle entered Ruth's faded blue eyes. "Do I pass muster?"

Kayla's gaze moved from the ridiculous straw hat crowning Ruth's short blond curls, over the youthful jungle-patterned skirt set, down her birdlike, blue-veined legs, to the pink canvas shoes on her feet. "You're looking very well," she said.

Despite the totally uncharacteristic outfit and hairstyle, Ruth *did* look well, although Kayla cautioned herself that her grandmother's healthy glow was probably illusory, merely the result of being in the sun for a week.

"Well, I'm *feeling* well," Ruth asserted, seemingly reading Kayla's doubts.

"You've lost weight."

"So have you. I had a heart attack. What's your excuse?"

"Hello, Kayla." Philip's greeting provided a welcome escape from Ruth's uncomfortable scrutiny. Still, as he extended his hand, Kayla's reserve returned, along with a strong current of animosity.

After a slight hesitation, she reached across the distance that divided them and shook his hand. She didn't say anything, however. She didn't even nod.

Philip had a firm grip, she reflected. An honest grip. Though that was probably an illusion, too.

She didn't really know Philip Reed, hadn't paid much attention to him those few times she'd gone with Ruth to his office. Matt had occupied all her attention back then. But she thought she remembered him as the quintessential accountant—mild-mannered, conservative, nose to the grindstone and fingers on the calculator. Apparently, her memory was faulty. "What's with the beard, Dad?" Matt's smile seemed strained.

"Don't you just love it!" Ruth exclaimed with girlish enthusiasm.

Matt's eyes cooled as they cut in her direction. "It's...different."

Kayla suspected Matt had never seen his father wearing sandals or a Hawaiian shirt, either. He'd withdrawn into a watchful uneasiness that she understood completely.

"Well, *I* like it," Philip maintained, determinedly undercombing his chin with his fingers. He and Ruth looked at each other and laughed softly, a private conversation riding on their linked gaze.

Kayla hadn't realized what a handsome man Philip was. He was almost as tall as his son, had a stunning head of thick hair, white to match his beard, and a twinkle in his gray eyes that gave him an air of Cary Grant joie de vivre.

Matt picked up his bags. "So, how far away is the house you're renting?"

"Not far. About a fifteen-minute drive," his father replied. They started toward the exit.

"Now, Kayla, you aren't going to run right to a phone and call your father, are you?" Ruth warned. "Before we go a step farther, you'll have to promise me that. Otherwise we might as well say goodbye right here."

Kayla gnawed on the corner of her lip. Finally she acquiesced. "All right. I won't call my father. I promise."

They stepped through a glass door Philip held open for them. Even at five-thirty, the sun hit like a blast from a furnace. Ruth cast a disparaging glance at Kayla's business suit. She'd taken off her jacket, but her blouse was still heavy silk, and long-sleeved.

"Whatever possessed you to wear something so warm, love?"

"I'm fine."

Ruth clucked her tongue, glancing at Matt's flannel trousers.

"I'm fine," he repeated with a touch of annoyance.

"Our rental car is parked in the lot across the road."

By the time they reached the vehicle, Kayla's clothes were glued to her. While Philip unlocked the trunk, she unbuttoned her sleeves and peeled them back.

Once the bags were stowed, they piled into the car, Ruth in the front with Philip, leaving the back seat to Matt and Kayla.

As they pulled into traffic, Matt sat up at sudden attention. "Whoa. They drive on the left here?"

His father chuckled. "Takes a little getting used to." Ruth turned, draping her age-spotted left arm over the seat. "You can't imagine how pleased I am you're here. I realize Freeport isn't Nassau, but it still has *so* much to offer. There are two huge casinos, exciting marketplaces, good food and music..."

"Gran, we didn't come here to take a vacation."

Matt supported her. "We can only spare a few days away from our jobs. We'd like to spend what little time we do have visiting with you."

Ruth wrinkled her nose girlishly, a gesture Kayla had never noticed before. "But that's ridiculous. I know you can't mean it. Oh, look." Her face lit with wonder. "Isn't that bougainvillea spectacular?"

Kayla and Matt cast disinterested glances in the direction Ruth was pointing.

"Very nice," Kayla murmured, but her gaze swung right back to her grandmother. She wasn't interested in the local flora. At the moment she was too busy studying the changes in Ruth, searching for the disturbing tendencies her father and brother had said she was exhibiting.

Kayla had other things on her mind, as well—like, how was she going to separate Ruth from Philip? And what would she say once she did have her grandmother alone? Meanwhile, Ruth was chattering on about casuarina trees and poincianas and something about gardens of... of groves? Kayla had never seen her grandmother so excited over vegetation before. Ruth's world had begun and ended with the walls of her factory.

Kayla shifted her gaze to the back of Philip's head. And how formidable a foe would Philip become once he understood her reason for coming here? She wasn't looking forward to confrontation, but confrontation seemed inevitable. She already regretted having promised not to call home. On the other hand, if the situation became dire enough, wouldn't not calling be irresponsible of her?

She realized slowly that Philip had taken up the travel commentary. She rested her head against the seat, shutting out his voice, trying to concentrate. If she was going to return to Boston on Wednesday, she had only tonight, tomorrow and Tuesday to accomplish her task. Not a lot of time by anybody's measure.

However, she couldn't rush things, either. She had to be cautious, nurturing the trust that existed between her and her grandmother now. Tonight she'd merely observe the situation, take note of the woman's health and habits and watch for signs of Philip's duplicity.

And Matt? She turned her head to look at him. What was his role going to be in all this?

Her inadvertent sigh drew him out of his thoughts, thoughts that seemed as deep and troubled as her own. Their eyes met, and her heart went suddenly tripping.

Oh, hell, she cursed to herself, feeling the tug of his masculine appeal. She pulled her gaze away, fixed it on the passing scenery and booted Matt Reed out of her thoughts. Her fragile ego deserved no less.

"This is it," Philip caroled. "Our home away from home."

The car passed through a gate in a pink stucco wall. At the end of a short driveway stood a matching pink stucco house, a two-storied affair with a red tile roof and a Mediterranean flavor.

"It's lovely, Gran."

"Isn't it just? It's right on the beach, too, and yet it's within minutes of everything—the Lucaya marketplace, the casino and big hotels..."

Philip parked the car and as they got out he added, "We have it for two more weeks."

"Then what?" Kayla asked, even though his reply didn't matter. Ruth would be back in Boston in a few days.

"We're not sure yet." Ruth's eyes danced. "Maybe we'll island hop, or maybe we'll fly off to Europe."

Kayla felt uneasy with the answer. She'd never known Ruth not to have an agenda.

The house was large, modern and airy, and decorated with cool rattan furniture, tropic-flowered cushions, sea-green carpeting and lots of sunshine. Broad expanses of glass looked out on a patio and lushly planted back lawn. Turquoise ocean glittered through the foliage at the property's far border.

Ruth opened one of the glass sliders and breathed deeply of the perfumed air that wafted in. "I never tire of waking to this."

Philip placed his hand on her shoulder and smiled down at her—rather too warmly, Kayla thought irritably." It's like living in paradise," he said, holding Ruth's bright gaze.

Matt cleared his throat. "Where shall we put our bags?"

"Slow down, Matthew." Philip chuckled. "You'll live longer." He then disappeared into the kitchen.

Meanwhile, Ruth lifted her straw hat and fluffed her blond curls. Over her left temple hung three tiny braids, each artfully entwined with colored glass beads.

"Gran, what on earth . . . ?"

"Oh, do you like my braids?" Ruth beamed until her cheeks shone.

"I . . . I don't understand."

"You will soon enough. You can't go anywhere without some charming local girl coming up to you and offering to braid your hair."

Kayla pressed a hand to her French twist, still neat after a full day of traveling. "Not my hair."

"Oh, Kayla!" Ruth shook her head, laughing. "You can't return to the States without getting at least a couple of braids."

Kayla was beginning to realize the futility of telling her grandmother she wasn't here on vacation.

"With your long hair, you'd look so exotic, too," Ruth added. "You do still have your long hair, don't you?"

As she nodded, Kayla felt an uncomfortable heat spill over her. Matt's dark head was tilted, and his eyes were surveying her in a way that made her feel like a commodity whose latent value he was trying to assess.

Just then Philip returned with a tray of festively garnished drinks. Rum drinks? Kayla wondered, giving the man a hostile look. Alcohol was definitely verboten when it came to Ruth's health.

Noticing her expression, he held the tray in front of her hesitantly. "You don't like papaya juice?"

"Oh." She fidgeted uncomfortably. "Yes. Yes, I do. Thank you." The man moved on, casting one last frown her way.

After they'd had a chance to unwind a bit, Matt and Kayla were led upstairs and shown to their rooms, decorated identically in turquoise and green. Ruth stayed with Kayla while she unpacked.

"Oh, Kayla! That isn't all you brought, is it?" Ruth exclaimed.

Kayla looked from the shorts she was tugging on to the skirt she'd hung in the closet. "I won't need much else. Really, this is plenty."

But her grandmother remained crestfallen.

"Blame it on my genes, Gran. Brayton frugality," Kayla tried to quip, but the appeal to family principles didn't work.

"No bathing suit? You can't be here without a bathing suit."

"Of course I can."

"Oh, no. We'll just have to put that on our list of things to buy when we go shopping tomorrow."

Kayla was about to protest again when she realized that here was the opening she'd been looking for. Shopping. Sure. Matt and Philip wouldn't be interested in accompanying her and Ruth on a clothes-shopping excursion. She'd have Ruth all to herself.

"I guess I did come unprepared." From out of nowhere, a warm, loving feeling welled up inside her. "I've really missed our shopping trips, Gran."

"Oh, pooh." Ruth waved her off. "I used to dress you like an old futz. It's a wonder you didn't run away from home. Come on, let's join the men."

Matt and his father were just stepping out to the corridor. Matt had changed into lighter clothing, too. As they headed for the stairs, Kayla realized there was only one other bedroom on this floor. Although no one commented, she felt awareness heavy in the air—Philip and her grandmother were sharing a room. The thought unsettled her in more ways than she cared to examine.

Descending the stairs, Philip said, "Would you believe this son of mine brought along a computer?" He

gave the back of Matt's head a playful cuff. Kayla was
relieved she hadn't unloaded *her* briefcase or she might
be receiving a similar reproof.

What had happened to these two once-sensible people?
Her grandmother had changed, not only in appearance
but in her attitude and mannerisms, as well. Was it senility? Were both afflicted, or was Philip merely leading
Ruth on? "That fish smells divine, Ruthie." Philip
breathed rapturously, ushering them into the well-
equipped kitchen.

"I can't take the glory tonight, Phil. Tanecia prepared
tonight's meal." Ruth took four plates from a cupboard
and handed them to Kayla, explaining, "Tanecia's the
young woman who comes in to clean and deliver
groceries. She's teaching me to cook a few island dishes."

Her grandmother cooking? Kayla's thoughts took
another spin.

"Is tonight's meal compatible with your diet, Gran?"
Ruth must've heard the censure in her voice because she
seemed mildly perturbed when she replied, "It's fish,
dear. Boiled. Of course, it's compatible."

Kayla took note of the defensiveness she'd stirred and
quickly changed the topic.

Conversation remained light throughout dinner, which
they ate outdoors on the patio. Yet Kayla noticed a
curious caution in the two older folks. She caught them
exchanging glances that made her uneasy. It wasn't until
they were having their after-dinner coffee, though, that
the reason was made known.

"Well, Ruthie—" Philip cast one of his debonair
smiles at the woman he was addressing "—I guess we've
danced around what's really on our minds long enough."

Matt was sitting to Kayla's right at the round glass
table. He slowly lowered his coffee. "And what exactly
is on our minds, Dad?"

His father met his narrowed stare. "Why Ruth and I are here. What else?" Tension thickened the silence that followed.

"You've claimed repeatedly you're here on vacation." Matt seemed to want his father to reaffirm that claim.

"We are," Ruth said carefully. "But it's more than that. Which is the reason *you're* here."

Kayla gulped. "Why *we're* here?"

"Yes. Oh, I don't mean the reason your father sent you." Ruth tossed her hand dismissively. "I mean the reason we let you come."

Kayla stammered unintelligibly for a few embarrassing seconds before she managed to say, "You *know* why Dad sent me?"

Ruth gave her one of her wry you've-got-to-be-joking looks that suggested her mind was as sharp as ever.

"Yet you still invited me?" Kayla asked. "Why?"

Ruth reached for Philip's hand. "Call us sentimental, but Phil and I decided we really would like to have family with us at our wedding."

His father met his narrowed stare. "Why Ruth and I are here, Winterset? Trusting Oil, that's the answer that follows."

"You've claimed supposedly that we have no salvation." Matt said to Ruth, as she started toward them.

CHAPTER FOUR

THEY seemed a tableau of garden statues, frozen within the shock of the moment.

"Wedding?" Matt finally repeated.

Kayla was struck simultaneously with two thoughts. Her father was probably right about Philip's wanting to get hold of Ruth's assets. And her father was probably wrong about Matt's complicity. His surprise at this moment was too real, his reaction too clearly negative.

"Yes, we're planning to be married." Philip cast Ruth a conspiratorial smile. "We've already made all the arrangements."

Ruth winked at him before turning to the younger people. "However, there's one detail of the ceremony we'd like to change."

Kayla snapped out of her stupor. "What's that, Gran?"

"We'd like you and Matt to be our attendants."

Matt sprang to his feet, glaring at his father. "Are you out of your mind?"

Philip's jaw hardened, but not before Kayla saw his pain. Ruth took his hand in both of hers.

Matt continued to glower. "Where the hell did the idea of marriage come from?"

"Surely it isn't that much of a surprise? Ruth and I have been seeing each other for months."

Matt thrust his fingers through his thick dark hair and began to pace. "You said you were just friends."

"We were. That's how things started."

"Things? *Things?* For heaven's sake, Dad, you're sixty-five years old, and she—" he pointed accusingly "—she's even older. What *things?*"

"Sit down, Matthew. You're making everyone nervous." Philip turned to Kayla. "What's your reaction to our news? Are you as opposed to it as he is?"

Even this morning Kayla would've laughed if anyone had suggested she and Matt Reed were allies, yet now she could only nod. "I'm sorry, but I agree with Matt."

"Oh, dear." Ruth's brow beetled. "We were hoping you, at least, would understand."

"What do you mean, me at least?"

"Well, being involved in a serious relationship. We thought you'd sympathize, you'd know what it's like to find the person you want to spend the rest of your life with."

A sudden quiver of nausea snaked up to Kayla's mouth. She passed an unsteady hand over her damp brow. "You aren't really trying to compare yourselves with me and Frank, are you?"

Ruth tilted her head, perplexed at first and then incensed. "Heaven forbid. What could two old dinosaurs like us possibly know about love? I forgot, you young people have a lock on the commodity, don't you?"

Matt whirled around, planting his hands hard on the back of his vacated chair. "Will you stop this nonsense about love! Sorry, Ruth. I've always admired you but, dammit, what are you doing to him?" His eyes shot to his father.

"Me? Doing to him? I don't follow."

Neither did Kayla. She looked on intently. Matt was a study in anger—knuckles white, chest rising and falling like a bellows—and yet some other emotion haunted his eyes, something that gave her the irrational urge to reach out and take his hand the way her grandmother had taken Philip's.

"My mother," Matt rasped. "That's what I'm talking about, Ruth. She's been gone barely a year." He gave the chair a hard shove and went back to pacing.

Ruth's mouth opened in a silent O as understanding dawned.

"Matthew!" Philip erupted. "You're out of line."

"Am I?"

"Positively. That was cruel and unnecessary. Inaccurate, too, if you've got me pegged as some lonely old fool who's..."

"Did I say fool?" Matt bellowed.

"No, but that's what you were thinking."

"What I was thinking was that Mom hasn't been gone all that long and you're still emotionally vulnerable."

"Emotionally vulnerable." Philip chuckled sardonically. "Emotionally vulnerable." But then he rolled the phrase around his tongue one more time, as if tasting something new in its syllables. "Yes, I suppose I am still emotionally vulnerable, unlike some people I know, and I thank God that I am."

The space between father and son vibrated with accusations Kayla wished she understood. She looked to her grandmother for a clue, but Ruth's eyes were lowered. One thing she did understand—she wished the men would cool off.

"Gran, have you thought this marriage thing through?"

"Thoroughly. I've known Phil for thirty-five years..."

"Which only makes me wonder why? Why *now?*"

"Who knows why now?" Ruth sighed. "Except that it has something to do with my heart attack."

"And with my losing my wife," Phil interjected.

"And with realizing life isn't a dress rehearsal."

Matt flung himself into a chaise in the shadows of the patio, muttering darkly.

"So, what are you saying, Gran? Your heart attack gave you a new perspective on life?" Kayla hoped her voice didn't reveal how trite she thought that particular line of reasoning was.

"It certainly did, Kayla. Carpe diem. That's my philosophy now." Ruth paused, "Oh, I can see you don't approve."

"Well...it sounds appealing, but if we all seized the day, I'm afraid civilization would come to a screeching halt. Nobody would show up for work or make sacrifices for the future or..."

"I wasn't implying we should be irresponsible, love, just open our eyes and our hearts to what makes us happy."

"Happy. And how happy do you think you made Dad when you disappeared last week?"

"Oh, pooh. That father of yours..."

"That *son* of yours. You don't think he was worried sick?"

"We had no choice, Kayla," Philip said, wrapping a possessive arm around Ruth's shoulders. Kayla glared at the arm, quivering with resentment.

"Lloyd turned my home into a prison," Ruth complained. "While I was in the hospital I signed a paper that gave him the authority to handle all my medical decisions, which was fine while I was in an emergency situation, but I never thought he'd continue after I went home."

Kayla frowned. "What did he do?"

"For one thing, he fired my cook and hired a...a dietician." Ruth's tone left no doubt about what she thought of the dietician's culinary skills. "He stuck me with a companion who bores me silly, stopped talking about the factory so I had to go out of my way to find out what was happening. Why, he even took away my driver's license."

Kayla realized her skepticism was showing when Philip said, "He really did, Kayla. He treated her like a total incompetent."

"My father was only looking out for her health." *Unlike you,* her scowl implied. "And you have no right to undermine his efforts. It's irresponsible and dangerous."

Ruth and Philip exchanged meaningful glances again. Damn, Kayla thought in dismay. Whenever they did that, they seemed to come away refortified.

"Please try to understand. Maybe Lloyd *was* acting out of concern for my health, but I felt so stifled, Kayla, so useless. And so very old."

Kayla had never heard her grandmother's voice crack before. It struck at her composure.

"Philip was my release, Kayla. My escape." Ruth gazed lovingly at the debonair, white-haired man beside her.

"At first my visits were merely courtesy calls," Philip explained. "But it didn't take long before I realized how much I enjoyed your grandmother's company."

"And, oh, did I enjoy his," Ruth said on a blissful sigh. "We played cards, put old records on the phonograph, talked and laughed for hours on end. We had so much in common. You know, life experiences that only we understood."

"When she got the green light from her doctor, I started to take her out."

"Unfortunately, the more we saw of each other, the harder Lloyd came down on me. He started pressuring me to transfer ownership of Brayton's to him. He wanted me to bequeath what was in my will before I was even gone. But the final straw was his suggestion I move into a nursing home. I couldn't take that, Kayla. Not that."

Kayla sprang to her feet and, like Matt a few minutes earlier, began to pace. "I...I don't believe it. Dad would never put you in a home."

"Oh, I know he wouldn't. He couldn't, unless he was able to somehow prove I was mentally incompetent, because he certainly can't prove I'm physically incompetent."

Kayla's skin prickled. Her father was already accusing Ruth of mental incompetency, but in private, among the family. Surely he didn't intend to do anything more...did he?

Ruth leaned forward, her expression almost desperate in its earnestness. "It just hurt so much to know that the idea of a nursing home had entered my son's mind. More than that, that he was actually trying to convince me that I belonged in one."

Ruth's faded blue eyes glistened with moisture. "I know I'm old, Kayla." Her lips trembled ever so slightly. "I don't need anyone to remind me I'm not the vigorous woman I used to be or that my days on this earth are numbered. I live with that reality all the time. That's precisely why I had to get away from Boston. I want to make the most of what little I have left. I've wasted too much of my life already." She lifted her determined aristocratic chin, even while a tear trickled down her wrinkled cheek. "With Philip I'll be free to do just that. Lloyd won't be able to touch me after we're married."

Silence descended as thick as the tropic night.

Suddenly Matt's deep, bitter voice rumbled from the shadows. "Why?"

Everyone turned, blinking distractedly.

"Why what, son?"

"I can understand why you kept your running off a secret from Lloyd Brayton, but why did you lie to me?" His voice scraped with anger and pain.

Philip sighed. "We didn't exactly lie."

"You did. You used me. You fed me a line about Ruth being harassed and needing a rest, and because you said you were only acting out of friendship, I helped you get away. I found you this place, I arranged your flight, drove you to the airport. I did it all without saying a word, even though I thought she was taking unfair advantage of your friendship." The look he cast Ruth suggested that his belief had only deepened. "Fool that I am, I even had a whopper of an argument with Lloyd Brayton when he dared voice a doubt about what you were really up to." Matt swore under his breath, his head jerking with each heartfelt epithet. "Why didn't you tell me you were planning to get married?"

Philip sighed. "I'm sorry, Matthew, but we didn't think you'd be any happier about our plans than...than you apparently are."

"And we didn't need any more opposition than we already had in Lloyd," Ruth added.

Matt's gaze slid away peevishly. "So when's this ceremony supposed to take place?"

Ruth's eyes softened with sympathy. "Tuesday. And as we said, we'd like you and Kayla to be our best man and maid of honor. It isn't necessary, of course. Witnesses are easy to find, but we'd really like them to be you. You're the dearest people in all the world to us."

Still pacing, Kayla gnawed on the inside of her cheek. Sitting in the shadows, Matt clutched his skull.

"Tell you what." Philip lit a thin cigar, puffed and studied the glowing tip. "We'll agree to put off the ceremony until, oh, say Thursday, if Kayla will agree not to call home with the news until it's over."

Kayla's eyes narrowed in renewed suspicion. And why would Philip be asking that?

"That'll give you two a few more days to work on us. You know, try and convince us of the reasons we shouldn't get married."

"And if any of our arguments make sense?" Matt inquired.

"We'll consider them. Seriously, we will. In the meantime we're hoping you'll come to know us better as a couple and in the end give us your blessing."

Not likely, Kayla thought. *Not bloody likely.* Slouched in his chaise, Matt seemed to be thinking the same.

"Well, if you'll excuse us now..." Ruth got to her feet and, noticing Kayla glance at her watch, explained, "These days, I turn in much earlier than I used to."

Arm in arm, the older couple retreated into the house, leaving Kayla and Matt to stew in their cauldron of muddled emotions alone.

And they did. For nearly ten full minutes, Matt brooded in his corner while Kayla stared in the vague direction of the ocean, arms knotted high and tight.

"They're sharing a room, you know," she finally muttered.

"I noticed. You don't suppose their going to bed early means that they're...?" Matt's mind seemed to shut down. As did Kayla's.

"It's my grandmother's health," she supplied quickly. "She needs more sleep these days."

"Of course."

Silence. Silence so still Kayla was sure Matt could hear her pounding heart.

"So, what are we going to do?" he asked, pushing up from the chaise.

"I don't know."

He stood with her at the edge of the patio, arms similarly folded, staring across the night-shadowed lawn toward a line of tall palm trees—dark, graceful curves painted on the lighter, almost opalescent silk of the sky.

"Want to go for a walk?"

Kayla sighed unenthusiastically. "Sure."

"Let me just get the gate key."

The property was walled on three sides, with a see-through wire fence bordering the beach. Native vegetation, including a copse of feathery casuarina trees, provided a screen for semiprivacy.

Matt unlocked the fence gate and opened it for Kayla to pass through. Under a three-quarter moon, the sand appeared the color and consistency of sugar. Feeling it sift into her shoes, Kayla pried them off.

"Mm. Feels good," she murmured, wiggling her toes. Matt removed his shoes, too. They continued on to the water's edge where they both looked up and down the beach. It was deserted.

It was also breathtaking. The sea was calm tonight, with just the softest of waves curling onto the sand. Moonlight silvered the entire panorama, creating a setting that seemed custom-made for postcard photographers—or for lovers.

With a small shake of her head, Kayla turned her errant thoughts to the situation at hand. "Did this marriage news surprise you as much as I think it did?" She waded into the water until she was knee-deep.

"Let's say the idea crossed my mind once or twice, but I never gave it serious attention. Yes, it surprised me. It really did." Matt rolled his pants legs and joined her in the water. After a while he said, "And you really didn't know what your father was doing to your grandmother?"

Kayla shook her head. "Tonight was the first I'd heard of it. I'm afraid we've both been used."

In silent accord, they began walking toward the lights beaming from a clutch of large hotels about a mile away.

"I'm sorry I snapped at your grandmother. She and I have always gotten along."

Kayla shrugged. "Believe it or not, I understand why you snapped. Your father probably *is* still emotionally vulnerable." Fleetingly the phrase reminded her of Philip's implication that Matt was *not*.

"Of course he is. He's lonely and he misses my mother and would do anything to have her back." Matt tucked his fingers into the back pockets of his trousers, pulling taut his cotton shirt across his broad chest.

"And you think my grandmother is simply an emotional Band-Aid."

"Yes. A Band-Aid, a substitute..."

"That very well could be." Kayla felt Matt's gaze on her.

"That's pretty big of you, admitting that you see my side."

"Not really. Once I realized how recently your mother had passed away, I totally understood."

Matt dragged a hand down his face. "Poor Ruth. She might not even realize what she's doing to my father." He walked on. "Then again, she might. She said it herself, my father is her escape. Married to him, she'll be free of Lloyd."

With an effort Kayla held back the remark that Philip had a great deal to gain from the union, too. More than Ruth did, in her estimation. But it was obvious that the love Matt bore his father didn't allow for anything nefarious in the older man's conduct, and seeing Matt so bothered by his own concerns, Kayla felt strangely reluctant to upset him with hers.

His voice was softer, wistful, when he said, "They had a wonderful marriage."

"Your father and mother?"

"Mm. In this crazy, ever-changing world they were so solid, so steady."

"That must've been very reassuring, growing up."

"It was. Most of the credit goes to my mother, though. She was always there for us, for me and my father. The house was always warm and welcoming, meals were gracious, and our clothes... well, let's just say we never went around with buttons missing. Not that I have anything against women working. Just the opposite. But there's something about a home that's well tended, a home with a woman in it..." His voice thinned. A scowl slid like a shadow over his expression.

Kayla wondered what he was thinking. She got the feeling his mind had wandered, that he was no longer thinking about his childhood home. Was it possible he was remembering his own marriage?

Abruptly, he flicked his head. "I'm sorry. Here I'm going on about my mother, and you never knew yours, did you?"

"No."

"Were you very young when she died?"

"You might say that. She didn't make it through childbirth."

Matt stopped walking. "Oh." Slowly he turned to gaze out over the water, eyes narrowed.

Kayla paused with him, standing close enough to feel his body heat shimmering like a charged electrical field along her side. Belatedly she remembered her resolution to watch what she did with Matt on this visit, a resolution that clearly precluded moonlit strolls on postcard beaches. Her vulnerable heart and fragile ego would suffer if she didn't use caution.

But at the moment her fears seemed rather irrelevant. This moonlit stroll had come about so naturally, and it seemed a *good* thing to be talking.

He asked quietly, "Is that why you're so close to Ruth?"

"Mm. She's the one who took me home from the hospital. My father couldn't cope with a newborn at that particular time in his life." But he could cope with a three-year-old, Kayla thought sadly. "I stayed with Ruth until I was four."

Matt looked at her, astounded. "It must've been pretty upsetting, moving into a strange house at that age."

"Not really. My grandmother had made sure I spent lots of time there. Meals, visits, sleep overs. And naturally I saw plenty of my father at the factory. She took me in to work with her almost every day."

"You spent your early childhood in a factory?" Matt asked with an incredulous laugh.

"Pretty much. It was great. All that room to zoom around on my tricycle." Out of nowhere, Kayla's eyes were stinging. "Oh, Matt, I don't know what to do. She sounds like her old rational self, but she's changed so much, too."

Unexpectedly Matt placed his hand, large and warm and reassuring, on her shoulder. "Physically she doesn't look bad. Really she doesn't," he insisted when she cast him a dubious look. "Neither does my father. But I understand your distress. It's the simple fact that they *have* changed. It's a sign that something more serious is going on under the surface."

Kayla nodded, feeling a slight loosening of the muscles where his fingers pressed. "That foolishness about carpe diem goes against the grain of her entire life." *My life, too,* Kayla thought. "In fact, it clashes with every principle our family values—setting goals, working hard, self-discipline, frugality."

"She's probably just running scared. Aging, nursing homes—those are pretty frightening prospects."

Kayla nodded. "Your father, too. Losing a lifelong mate can't be easy."

Matt removed his hand from her shoulder. "Well, whatever the reasons, I take it you agree with me that their getting married is a mistake."

"Absolutely. Under the best of conditions marriages between elderly people are chancy."

"Definitely. They're set in their ways. They're carrying a lifetime of emotional baggage. So many handicaps."

"And these are hardly the best of conditions." She lowered her head, staring at the waves gently foaming about their ankles. "Matt, I'm sorry my father and brother were so quick to accuse you of conspiring to rob us of Brayton Clocks." The full implications were just dawning on her. If word of those accusations spread, Matt's reputation, and hence his business, would be ruined, unjustly so. It was no wonder he'd been so angry.

He shrugged. "Obviously you people have seen this marriage issue coming for a while. I'm not surprised you were so quick to blow. I would've been, too. Good Lord, if Ruth marries my father..." His voice thinned. "Her stocks and bonds... her position at Brayton's..." Implications seemed to be just dawning on him, too.

Kayla gripped her head in two hands and emitted a strangled cry. "What are we going to do, Matt?"

"I'll tell you one thing I'm *not* going to do—that's be their best man."

"And I refuse to be their maid of honor."

"Good." Taking her elbow, he turned and started back the way they'd come. "What we've got to do is make the most of the reprieve they've given us."

"Yes. The two extra days."

Matt growled in vexation. "That'll mean being stuck here until Thursday night or Friday."

"More reshuffling of schedules."

"Nearly a whole week's worth."

"Matt?"

"Hm?" His hand drifted to her shoulder again, sending a delightful shiver skimming over her skin. She ignored it, though, telling herself his touch was merely that of a friend, a friend who coincidentally shared the same problem.

"What if we can't change their minds?"

"We will. We have to. Nothing good can come of this marriage."

Kayla nodded. "My grandmother and I have plans to go shopping tomorrow. I'll talk to her then."

"Good. And while you're gone, I'll talk to my father."

They smiled at each other, their steps coming to a stop in the surf. Quite suddenly Matt dipped his head and kissed her, quickly, chastely. Nevertheless, the move left her breathless.

"What was that for?"

He shrugged. "To seal our pact. To express relief that we're not sniping anymore. I honestly don't know." And just for a second he did look puzzled. But then he smiled. "Maybe I just wanted to see something in those pretty blue eyes of yours besides worry." His eyes danced with devilment.

Apprehension flowed over her, along with something that felt too much like pleasurable excitement. Was he flirting with her?

No. Of course he wasn't. Of course not. He was smiling that smile merely because he was amused by her. Evidently he still thought of her as young and awkward, still enjoyed baiting her and seeing her get flustered. If anything, she should be annoyed by the arrogance and condescension implicit in such an attitude.

Before she could think of a proper response, though, he said, "Come on, let's get back to the house," and started walking up the beach.

That night, after washing and changing into her nightgown, Kayla decided to call Frank. Sitting on the double bed in her room, she was somewhat amazed that she hadn't given him a thought all day except when Matt had asked about him.

Ah, well, so much had happened today, she supposed her negligence was forgivable.

They didn't talk long—Frank kept reminding her of the cost of the call—but they did manage to catch up on most of the news of their day. He filled her in on store sales. She told him about her flight and the weather and her assessment of Ruth's health. She even disclosed their location, laughing over how obvious it was, then making him swear to keep the information a secret. What she didn't tell him, though, was that Ruth and Philip planned to be married in a few days. She wasn't sure why.

After hanging up, Kayla lay back on the bed's soft pillows. It had been good hearing Frank's voice, she told herself. Grounding. It reminded her of who she was and what her life was about. For some reason she seemed to especially need that reminder tonight.

But when she tried to conjure up Frank's image, only fragments came to mind. His sandy hair. The curve of his chin. A tie he favored. It was frustrating that she couldn't pull any of the fragments together.

On the other side of the wall, from the bathroom she shared with Matt, came the sound of water splashing in the shower. Kayla closed her eyes as if that might turn off the sound. It didn't. What it did was sharpen the images that had begun invading her mind as soon as she'd realized who was in there.

Groaning in self-disgust, she flung herself under the covers and snapped off the light—only to find herself besieged by flickering images of the day—Matt comforting her through her fear of flying, Matt talking about his marriage, Matt brooding on the patio, Matt walking with her on the beach . . . and all the expressions that had moved over his handsome face, all the words that had fallen from those firm, gorgeous lips. She was dismayed that those images were so vivid and complete.

And now this—warm, soapy water sluicing down a wide, muscled back.

Kayla grabbed a pillow and jammed it over her head, smothering another groan. It was going to be a very long week. A very long week, indeed.

CHAPTER FIVE

ALTHOUGH Kayla was exhausted, she awoke early. Her neck muscles were already knotted, and her mind was charting out plans for the day.

The house was still. Moving as quietly as possible, she took a quick shower, blow-dried her hair and pinned it up in its usual twist. After applying a light but careful dusting of makeup, she slipped on her new white shirt, tied the green skirt in place, stepped into her flats and tiptoed out the door.

She found Matt sitting at the patio table, reading a newspaper. "Oh. I thought I was the first one up."

He lifted his eyes, and she said, "Oh," again. Why, she wasn't sure, except that his presence always seemed to strike a chord of wonder in her.

"Morning. Care for some coffee?"

"Yes, thank you." She pulled out a chair.

The table was laden with a plate of sliced fruit, a basket of sticky buns and an insulated carafe of coffee.

"Did you do all this?" she asked, accepting a cup from him.

"No, it was the girl who comes in to help. She was here earlier, dropped off some groceries, a few prepared dishes."

Kayla glanced away, unable to handle the thorough way his gaze was traveling over her. "Have you seen the two lovebirds yet?"

"Uh, no. They're still asleep." In disgust, he pushed the newspaper toward her. "Here. It's three days old, but you're welcome to it."

"Thanks. At least the local news will be different."

The sun had risen halfway up the eastern sky by the time Philip and Ruth made an appearance. Kayla had read the paper, washed breakfast dishes, paced the patio and finally turned to reading her trade magazine. Matt had reached his frustration level, too, and retrieved his computer from his room. When the older couple waltzed out to the patio, he was deeply immersed in composing a company newsletter.

"What a glorious morning!" Ruth threw back her head and took a rapturous breath. "The air is like champagne today."

"Mmm," Philip agreed. "Will you catch a whiff of those gardenias!"

Kayla looked up from her magazine. What gardenias?

"Morning," she said. "Would you like some breakfast?"

"In a bit. Phil and I are in the habit of taking a swim before we eat." They were each wearing beach robes. "Would you care to join us? You could improvise and wear your shorts, I suppose."

"No thanks, Gran. I have some reading to do."

"You, Matthew?"

Matt barely looked up from his computer long enough to shake his head.

The old people exchanged disparaging glances before shrugging and continuing toward the beach.

Apparently they'd become used to leisurely, almost formless mornings. They swam, they ate, they walked the beach looking for shells, and for about half that time, Matt and Kayla attended to their work. But finally impatience got the better of them and they went down to the beach, too, where they sat fully dressed in the shade of a palm tree, watching their elders' youthful antics and wondering when the *hell* they were going to start their day.

The morning wasn't without its diversions, though. Down the beach, offshore of the large hotels, the water was alive with activity—tour boats chugging out to the snorkeling reefs, inflated banana boats bouncing their laughing riders, jet-skis sending up sprays as they careened, and in the sky, a half dozen parasailers. Kayla watched the activity in the distance, somewhat intrigued, but mostly feeling disconnected from it.

"Gran, when are we going shopping?" she couldn't help asking when Ruth and Philip came out of the water after their second dip. She'd asked that question earlier and been told there was no rush; they were on island time, remember? But, heavens, it was now almost noon.

Ruth snatched her watch from the towel Kayla occupied. "I guess we should get a move on, Phil."

Kayla blinked. "I thought...aren't we going alone, Gran?"

Ruth squeezed water from her tight blond ringlets. "Why would we do that? The international bazaar is too much fun to leave anyone behind."

Kayla and Matt shot each other apprehensive glances.

"I thought I'd stay here at the house and keep my father company," Matt said.

"But Philip is going shopping, too." Ruth's tone implied that anyone with half a brain would've taken that fact for granted.

"I'm not sure that's such a good idea, Gran. The men are bound to be bored."

"Not at all," Philip protested amiably.

There was no way around it. They were all going shopping.

Even from the car park Kayla could see that the ten-acre marketplace was congested with tourists. She rolled her eyes. Matt silently commiserated with a similarly tortured expression.

They followed the older couple through the dramatic Japanese torii gate at the entrance to the bazaar and for over two hours strolled along cobblestone streets and tree-shaded courtyards, visiting several of the seventy-odd shops representative of more than thirty countries.

There was nothing either Kayla or Matt wanted to buy, however—except when they spotted a newspaper kiosk.

"I don't believe this!" Matt groused, after rifling the stand. "I can't find a paper less than two days old."

His father laughed. "Generally, that's as current as newspapers get here."

"Island time," Kayla muttered disparagingly.

It was mid-afternoon by the time Kayla finally found herself alone with Ruth. They'd come upon a women's clothing store that carried a wide selection of swimwear, and after she'd given Matt an eloquent elbow in the ribs, he'd claimed to be dying of thirst and succeeded in hauling his father off to a nearby pub.

Alone with her grandmother, Kayla twirled a circular rack of colorful bathing suits, searching for a tactful approach to the problem on her mind.

"So," Ruth said, smiling mischievously, "now that Phil's been shanghaied, what is it you want to discuss with me?"

Kayla's eyes snapped up.

Her grandmother laughed. "You never were able to hide anything from me, Kayla."

"Gran, can you be honest with me? I mean, really honest?"

"I'll try." Ruth held up a fluorescent pink bikini. "Oh, this is darling."

Kayla ignored it. "Why do you want to marry Philip?"

"Why?" She chuckled. "The usual reasons."

"Last night you seemed awfully upset about Dad's suggestion you consider moving to a nursing home, and, well, I can't help wondering if that isn't more the reason."

Ruth returned the bikini to the rack. "I know it's hard for someone your age to believe that someone my age can be in love, but I am, Kayla. I love Phil, and I'm in love *with* him, as well."

"And does he feel the same about you?"

"Why, I believe so."

"Are you sure?"

Ruth's lips compressed into a hard line. "What are you getting at, Kayla?"

Kayla moved on to a rack of filmy gauze skirts. "Well, it's just so sudden, and considering your resistance to signing over Brayton's to Dad..."

"Kayla, all my affairs are in order—my will, the corporation charter..."

"I know, but—" she gulped "—wills and charters can be changed."

Ruth looked startled. Her eyes widened. "You think Phil is marrying me with the intention of getting me to include him in my will?"

Kayla squirmed. "Well..."

Ruth's face abruptly hardened. "In other words, you think he's only marrying me for my money."

"Well..." Heat slid up Kayla's neck.

"Kayla, Phil doesn't need my money."

"Maybe not. But as the saying goes, you can never be too thin or too rich."

After a prickly silence, Ruth sighed. "Oh, Kayla. I suspected that was the reasoning behind your father's actions, although he never admitted it outright, but I never thought you would—"

"Answer one question, Gran. Whose idea was it to run away without telling anyone?"

The old woman's brow puckered. "I believe it was Phil's, but—"

"And marriage?"

"Phil proposed, of course. I'm not that liberated. But you can hardly jump from that to the conclusion he's after my money. Kayla, he knew I was tired of being watched and followed and censured. He knew I wanted to get away to a place where I could relax with him. And he knew I wanted to be married without family rancor spoiling our day. That's why we were so secretive. If I'd known I was going to get so much negativism from you, I never would've invited you here."

Tears stung Kayla's eyes with complete surprise. A salesgirl looked over. "Can we get out of here, Gran?"

"Gladly."

Ruth had barely stepped outside when she implored, "Is it so much to ask that you trust my judgment? Phil is a good man, Kayla. I trust him with my life, never mind my wealth. Can't you trust him, too?"

Kayla ground the toe of her shoe into a crack in the cobbles. "Maybe it isn't a question of trusting or not trusting Philip. Maybe..." She set her pained gaze on a store window glittering with Colombian emeralds. "Maybe what's got us worried is you, Gran, your casual disregard for the danger Brayton Clocks might be in, for the blithe way you're ready to put it in jeopardy. You know, the risk you're taking with your position as chairman of the board."

Every phrase seemed to straighten Ruth's spine further.

"Don't you know me well enough to realize I'd never do that? Can't you trust that I know what's good for the business and our family? That's all I want, Kayla— trust, confidence that I'm not a useless old woman who can't think for herself any longer."

"Fine. Then all you have to do is resign your chair. That'll prove to us that Brayton Clocks is secure in the family. Once you do, everyone will rejoice in your marriage."

Ruth's thin nostrils flared. "Do you hear what you just said?"

Kayla frowned. "Ye-es. What?"

"What! You've become as myopic as your father and brother. Your only concern is the business, not me, not my health or my happiness. In essence, what you're saying is, 'Fork over Brayton's, and we don't care what else happens to you.'"

"You're twisting things."

"Am I?"

Kayla's throat felt raw and tight. "Yes. We're *very* worried about you. Your doctors are nearly two thousand miles away. We have no idea if you're even taking your medication or following your diet."

Ruth threw up her hands. "Another sign that you think I've become an addle-brained old fool. I guess you think the changes in my appearance are a sign that I've gone soft in the head, too."

Kayla grew feverish. She'd planned to be a paradigm of tact, but somehow the wrong words had just begun spilling out.

"Laying aside the fact that I just plain like my new hairdo," Ruth continued, "has nobody considered the fact that it's a lot easier to care for than my old style? Kayla, I don't have time to be washing long hair or fussing with pins and hair spray. Sometimes I don't think I even have the strength in my arms. What's more, I feel pretty these days. Feminine. Oh, scoff if you want, but—"

Just then Kayla spotted Matt and his father standing about twenty feet away. Matt had intended to talk some sense into his father, too, but from the tight-lipped word fire they were exchanging, she surmised he wasn't doing any better than she was.

"What a pair you two make. Pathetic." Shaking her head, Ruth glanced from Matt to Kayla. "Come on. I need to rescue Phil."

When the men saw the women approaching, they swallowed their argument but remained sullen and glaring.

"Phil, I think I'd like to leave now." Ruth was breathing hard, and Kayla realized her grandmother was more angry now, seeing Philip upset, than she'd been over being attacked herself. Her eyes blazed with protectiveness as she stood by him.

"I was just thinking the same thing," he said, just as angry, just as protective. "This might be a good time to take the Martins up on their invitation."

"Wonderful. As long as we can leave these two behind. Let them find some other folks to make miserable."

Philip took Ruth's arm. "I was running out of conversation, anyway."

"Yes, and quite frankly their company bores me." They began to walk away.

"Gran!" Kayla's voice leapt with incredulity. "Gran, stop!"

Ruth turned. "What?"

"Where are you going?"

"To a resort in Lucaya. We met a couple from Boston who asked us to have dinner with them some time."

"But..."

"Oh, yes, silly us." The mockery in Ruth's angry voice made Kayla cringe. Ruth dug into her straw bag, then tossed Matt a house key. "A taxi can take you home. You remember the address, don't you?"

"Yes, but—"

"By the way," Philip interrupted, "we arranged a snorkeling trip for the four of us tomorrow. But if you don't want to go, seeing as how you're not here on vacation," he drawled sarcastically, "fine, stay home. Play with your computers and fax machines if that's what makes you happy. But we're going.''

''Gran, what about shopping for a bathing suit?''

''Kayla, you're a big girl. You can buy a bathing suit by yourself. Or not. Which is what you really prefer. Come on, Phil. We've wasted enough of our time with these two stiffs.''

Stunned, Kayla watched her grandmother walk off with Philip. ''I don't think I've ever been dismissed so thoroughly.'' Her voice scratched with humiliation and pain.

Wearing a look of matching astonishment, Matt pushed two hands through his hair and curled his fingers over his skull. ''I feel like an unwanted dog, pushed out of a car and abandoned on a country road.''

''Sh-should we go after them and apologize, do you think?''

He dropped his arms, expelling a shuddering breath. ''No. Let's let them cool. I think they really prefer—'' he paused and swallowed ''—they prefer not to be with us.''

Tears burned in Kayla's throat. ''I feel so rotten. I honestly didn't mean to say the things I did, but once I got going...''

''I know what you mean.''

''And now she doesn't want to be with me. What *have* I become?''

Matt's left eyebrow lifted in a silent question.

''Ruth accused me of only worrying about Brayton's, and I'm beginning to think she's right. I've been a royal pain in the rump since I got here.''

''So have I, but let's not be too hard on ourselves. Basically our hearts were in the right place.''

She cast him a doleful look.

"Okay, so we haven't been model houseguests, but we've had other things on our minds. Them, for instance. Their well-being."

"I do love her, you know." Kayla blinked at the sky, hoping the hot sun would evaporate the moisture gathering in her eyes.

Matt hooked an arm around her neck and pulled her to him. The move was unexpected but, oh, so welcomed. She buried her face in his shirtfront, fighting her billowing sadness. Her slender frame shook with the effort.

Matt pressed his lips to her ear. "It's okay, sweetheart. Sometimes it's all right to let go."

She groaned. Why did he have to go and say *that?* She gritted her teeth, but tears sprang to her eyes anyway. "I'm sorry. This is so unlike me. I don't know what's wrong."

"Not pregnant, are you?"

She pulled back, sadness giving way instantly to offense. "Of course not."

"It was a joke, Kayla."

"Oh." Her shoulders slumped. "What *have* I become? I don't even have a sense of humor anymore."

"Hey, it wasn't much of a joke, hardly worth getting upset over." His hands stroked her arms caressingly. His kindness—his *friendship*—touched her.

"Here." He handed her his handkerchief with a gentle smile.

She dabbed her eyes and glanced around, suddenly remembering they were standing in the middle of a busy thoroughfare in a crowded bazaar. Several people were giving them curious looks.

"Let them wonder," Matt said with a dismissive shrug. "Most will probably just think we're lovers who've had a quarrel."

"Oh, I don't think so."

Matt framed her face with his hands and held her mesmerized with his warm gray eyes. "No?" he asked softly, his thumbs stroking her hot cheeks. Alarms began to ring, but for the life of her, Kayla couldn't move away.

Slowly he lowered his head until his lips touched hers, brushing them, tantalizing them. "Yes, they will," he whispered. Then, angling his head, he pressed his mouth to hers. Unlike the brief, innocent kiss they'd shared the previous night, this one lingered. His lips were warm and pliant and much too capable, she realized, as her body began to respond.

This shouldn't be happening, she thought. Matt had never been attracted to her—she'd been too young, too unbecoming—and just like that kiss ten years ago, this one was born out of pity and compassion, too. Besides, she had Frank.

But that didn't stop the hot shivers from cascading over her skin. And it didn't keep her from kissing him back, tasting again the fantasy she thought she'd outgrown with her braces.

Only when his lips parted hers and the kiss deepened, sending an arrow of heat right to the core of her, did common sense return. Good Lord, what was she doing? She pulled back, mortified.

Matt's eyes opened slowly, their gray depths dark with arousal and something more. Surprise? "Yes, they'll definitely think we're lovers now," he whispered.

Kayla felt her cheeks blazing and looked away. But slowly, gradually, a traitorous smile eased over her frown. Even if he had kissed her simply out of pity, it was gratifying to know he'd been a little shaken, too.

Matt cleared his throat. "Well," he drawled, grinning and scratching the back of his head.

"Yes, well..." she echoed, grinning and rocking on the soles of her shoes. She looked around the square, again becoming aware of her surroundings. But this time everything seemed just a little different.

She blinked, wondering why she'd never heard those exotic birdcalls before, or seen the bright hues in those flowers, or smelled the spicy aroma wafting from that food cart. She blinked again, turning a half circle. It was like watching a black and white movie becoming colorized right before her eyes.

"Matt?" Did her voice really lilt?

"Mm?"

"Know what?"

"What?"

"I think we're in the Bahamas."

His grin spread. "That right?"

"Yeah. Look."

He obliged her, turning this way and that. "Well, I'll be damned."

"Know what that means, don't you?"

His eyes glittered as he smiled at her. "What?"

"I've got to get me a bathing suit."

CHAPTER SIX

MATT was a pleasure to shop with, although his taste in ladies' swimwear ran to the ridiculously skimpy. Kayla blithely ignored his choices and purchased a sensible blue maillot instead.

With that chore done, they decided to explore the straw market just beyond the international bazaar. Having spent most of the day squinting and feeling her skin tighten under the hot Bahama sun, Kayla had come to the grudging conclusion that those wide-brimmed hats her grandmother and Philip wore weren't really so silly after all.

The straw market was a ramshackle collection of old wooden stalls, crammed with merchandise inside and out—hats and bags, T-shirts, coral jewelry, postcards, wind chimes, key chains, coffee mugs, conch shells—myriad items guaranteed to tempt any tourist.

But the real delight, Kayla soon decided, was not the merchandise itself but the Bahamian women selling it. What a friendly, talkative people they were! Their melodic tones rose from every stall as they worked, weaving colorful raffia into their bags, beckoning passing shoppers with, "Come in and take a look, honey. Don't cost to look."

After browsing through several stalls, Kayla decided on a hat with a modest brim and a blue cotton sash that exactly matched her new bathing suit.

"Very tasteful," Matt commented dryly, even as he donned a large, open-weave panama with a garish

flowered band and tugged it low over his eyes. Kayla
burst out laughing.

He pretended to be offended. "Hey, I like it."

"You look like you just tumbled off a banana boat."

"That settles it, then."

He placed both their hats on a table heaped with
sweatshirts. "How much?"

The elderly vendor eyed him shrewdly, then quoted a
price.

Matt shook his head. He even backed away a couple
of steps before countering with a figure half what she'd
quoted. The vendor snickered, but came back with
another price.

Kayla watched the bargaining process with deepening
fascination. Matt wasn't just skilled at it, he was
charming, and by the time the deal was done she could've
sworn the old woman was openly flirting with him.

The woman's reaction reminded Kayla of the careful
restraint she had to exert in this man's presence. He was
uncommonly handsome and personable, and she had a
history of vulnerability to that appeal. She'd already
made one mistake today by allowing that kiss to happen
and couldn't afford to make another.

There was Frank, of course, the man who was waiting
for her in Chicago. But even if Frank didn't exist, Kayla
had to guard against giving away her heart to Matt, even
just a little. He hadn't meant anything by that kiss—a
gesture of friendship, a consolation when she'd been
troubled, nothing more—and if any sparks had ignited,
they'd merely been the automatic physical response he
would've felt with any woman. He was a healthy, virile
male, after all. She shouldn't read anything more into
it.

Another thing she had to remember was he was content
in his bachelorhood. Although he enjoyed the company
of women, nothing ever came of that company, and cer-

tainly nothing could come of hers. They lived a thousand miles apart. Next year they'd be even farther.

No, she'd made a mistake, but she wouldn't do it again.

Wearing their new hats, they left the straw market and wandered up the boulevard to the Princess Casino, a large, fantastical structure with Moorish spires and a Taj Mahal dome.

"I only want to peek," Kayla insisted. "I'm not a gambler."

"Me, neither. But it might be interesting to watch other people."

They went inside.

"I didn't expect so much noise." Kayla laughed. "What are all those bells?"

"I believe they're coming from the slot machines. They ring every time they pay off."

"Ah." Kayla gazed over the bright, colorful lights dancing and flashing everywhere. She hadn't expected those, either. "Wow," she said quietly.

With a hand at the small of her back, Matt ushered her forward. "Mind if I get a drink first?"

"Not at all. I'm pretty parched myself."

At the bar, he ordered a Kalik, the local beer, while Kayla got a frothy rum concoction called a Bahama Mama. Drinks in hand, they joined the noisy, dazzling activity.

Brimming with curiosity, Kayla strolled by Matt's side, taking it all in—clacking roulette wheels, nimble-fingered blackjack dealers, elegant baccarat tables and intense dice shooters. But the predominate attraction by far was the slot machine. There had to be hundreds of them here.

Kayla realized she was eyeing them with more than passing curiosity when she heard Matt's deep rumbling laugh and turned to find him holding out a quarter.

"Go on, give it a shot," he urged.

Automatically she shook her head. "No, thanks." She almost added, *I'm not here on vacation.* But then she paused, wavered and finally said, "Oh, why not?"

She stepped up to a machine feeling very much out of place. The people around her looked like old pros. They were planted on stools with plastic buckets of money between their knees, inserting coins as regularly and unemotionally as robots.

With a jump in her pulse, she slipped in the coin, pulled the lever and watched the symbols revolve— cherries, lemons, bananas. When they stopped, she continued to stare, waiting, until Matt said, "Put in another quarter."

She blinked. "I lost?"

"Yes. Put in another quarter."

"I *lost?*"

He laughed. "Yes."

Grumbling, she dug into her purse and inserted another coin. But the results were no better this time than the first. Kayla lost a dollar and fifty cents before she abandoned the machine.

"What a waste. No wonder they're called one-armed bandits."

Matt smiled at her with more warmth that she cared to notice. "Mind if I try my hand at blackjack?" he asked.

She shrugged. "It's your money."

Matt lost the first three deals he participated in, and at twenty dollars a deal, Kayla was beginning to sweat for him. She couldn't understand why he didn't wager the minimum. Five dollars seemed more than enough to gamble away. But Matt remained calm and won the fourth hand. He also won the fifth, then wisely walked away.

"Matt, look!" Kayla suspected she was glowing. "Five-cent slot machines. Now that's my kind of gambling."

She bought a two-dollar roll of nickels, found a money bucket and, feeling right at home, confidently started pumping in coins. Matt, meanwhile, manned a quarter machine back-to-back with hers. The first time the bells shrilled and nickels spewed forth, she thought she'd faint from excitement.

"How much?" Matt called out.

"Two dollars! Oh, wow!"

They each hit several times, but eventually, as was inevitable, the machines won out.

"Let's get out of here," Matt said, coming around to her side. "This place is addictive."

"And dangerous," she lamented, still perched on her stool, eyeing the three lonely nickels at the bottom of her bucket.

Matt gripped her under the elbows and lifted her bodily.

"All right, I'm coming, I'm coming," she said with a giggle.

When they stepped outside, Kayla was surprised to see that the sun had almost set. She'd been having so much fun she'd lost track of time.

Matt glanced at his watch. "Are you hungry?"

"Now that you mention it..."

"Do you want to go back to the house?"

"Why bother? No one will be there." Remembering the argument that had led to the older folks' abandoning them, Kayla's spirits deflated.

"And even if they were," Matt added, "they'd probably eat separately anyway."

"You're right. Let's give them more time to cool."

"Besides, if we eat out, we'll have more to tell them tomorrow. They'll like that, the fact that we've been doing touristy things."

Yes, the old folks would like that, Kayla thought. And they needed time to cool. *That* was why she and Matt weren't returning to the house just yet.

But Kayla was too smart not to know an excuse when she heard one, and the thing that was beginning to disturb her was, she wasn't the only one concocting the excuses.

Although there were several restaurants in the international bazaar area, she and Matt decided to take a bus to Port Lucaya because Ruth had raved about a restaurant there. It was also closer to the house, probably just over a mile along the beach. If they couldn't find a cab, they could always walk home.

They found the restaurant easily. It was within the Lucaya marketplace on Bell Channel Bay. From its second-story, open-air porch Kayla and Matt could watch the boating activity below at the marina and hear the music that drifted from the central square.

Studying her menu, Kayla said, "I suppose we should order something native."

Matt nodded. "I'm going to get the barbecued ribs."

"And I'll try the grouper. Looks like everything comes with peas and rice." They'd been introduced to the side dish at lunch, the hearty dark rice and brown peas that were an island staple.

After placing their orders and being served complimentary Bahama Mamas, Kayla sat back contentedly. The westering sun was gilding Matt's quickly tanning face and throwing highlights into his straight dark hair. For a moment Kayla couldn't help admiring him. He was such a visual treat.

But why was he studying her with such disquieting interest? What was going on behind those piercing gray eyes?

On a wave of self-consciousness, she turned and gazed out over the marina to where a glass-bottom boat was being hosed down for the night. Strains of "Island Boy" drifted from the square. The sky was streaked with shades of lavender and pink. And there—a tiny rainbow.

Kayla sighed, still finding it hard to believe she was where she was and not in Chicago, fighting ice storms and traffic. Inadvertently she smiled. Maybe it really didn't matter so much that newspapers were two days old or service was slow and the answer to every adversity was, "No problem, mon."

Or maybe... maybe her mellowing attitude had more to do with the company she was keeping.

"You'd better get a stronger sun block," Matt commented.

She turned at the sound of his voice. "Am I burned?"

"A little. Your nose, and here." He reached across the table and brushed her cheekbone.

"Ugh. How bad? Like a lobster?"

"No. Looks good, actually." His gaze stroked her face. His smile curled her toes.

No, this wouldn't do at all, she admonished herself. It was just such reactions that could get her into trouble.

She scowled at the white linen tablecloth and tried to feel businesslike. "So, what are we going to do about Ruth and Philip? What's the plan of action?"

Matt gazed off thoughtfully. "I haven't changed my mind about their getting married."

"Me, neither."

"But apparently we've got to try a different approach."

"What?" Kayla sipped her drink.

"Maybe we can persuade them to just live together?"

Kayla choked on an abrupt laugh. "My grandmother will never go for that."

"She's changed, Kayla. I'm going to give it a shot."

"Well, whatever we decide, we shouldn't argue with them."

"Agreed. We'll make no progress that way, only alienate them further." Matt traced an invisible pattern on the tablecloth with his thumbnail. "Maybe we should consider going on that snorkeling trip tomorrow."

"I've been thinking the same thing. Not that I really care to, but it'll make them happy."

"And if they're happy, they'll be more likely to listen to reason."

Their meal was served then, and they turned their attention to their food.

Surprisingly, dinner conversation grew lively. Kayla had never considered herself a great conversationalist, but tonight she talked torrents. So did Matt.

Not that she ever felt completely comfortable or relaxed. Quite the opposite, she always seemed short of breath, her cheeks flushed, and her body remained poised on the edge of her seat. But whatever this tension was, it was a joyous, exhilarating thing.

She was lost in a retelling of some anecdote from her college days when she suddenly realized Matt was staring at her. He was leaning forward, with his chin on his palm, and his eyes burned with such intensity that she forgot what she was saying and blushed right to her hairline.

He released her with a laugh. "I'm sorry. I know I've been staring and making you uncomfortable, but I can't help it. You have the most expressive face I've ever seen."

"Expressive?"

"Mm. It never stops moving."

Reflexively, Kayla half-covered her face with one hand. "Thanks. You make me feel like a blob of jelly." From the way his eyes lit, she suspected her face was doing something else again.

"I have to say, though, that it doesn't jibe with the hairdo or the clothes you usually wear."

"What do you mean?" She had to concentrate to string even those few words together. His steady gaze was making mincemeat of her brain.

"Well, there's a contradiction between your outer appearance and your expressiveness. One is polished and mature, the other's spontaneous and youthful. And I can't help wondering which is more the real you."

She lowered her head, but he reached over and tipped up her chin. "There's another reason I've been staring at you all day. I was right ten years ago. You've grown up to be one very beautiful woman."

Recalling when he'd made that prediction, Kayla bit her lip. Slowly she eased back from his touch.

"You have," he insisted, mistaking the cause of her embarrassment.

"Matt, about that date we had ten years ago..."

When she paused, wondering why in blazes she'd introduced that uncomfortable topic, he urged her on with, "What about it?"

"I've wanted to apologize to you ever since."

"Why, for heaven's sake?"

"Oh, you know." She couldn't meet his gaze.

Matt smiled softly. "It wasn't as bad as you think."

"Come on. You were so much older than me, a senior in college, and so popular. You had different interests and a serious girlfriend, and I...I was a total geek. You must've been mortified to be seen with me."

Her forthrightness threw him. He opened his mouth, closed it, opened it again and then laughed. "I'll admit I was a little uncomfortable, but only because we didn't know each other well."

"Hardly at all."

"But," he added, growing serious, "I was never embarrassed to be seen with you."

"But my braces, my hair and that awful red velvet dress."

He shrugged as if those things had slipped his memory. "Do you want to know what I remember most about that night?"

She clenched herself. "What?"

"I remember talking to you about our families' businesses, about Gustav Mahler and World Cup Soccer, and thinking you were one of the most interesting people I'd ever met."

Kayla's eyes widened.

"It's true," he said. "I also remember you had the longest repertoire of corny jokes I'd ever heard."

She pressed her palms to her burning cheeks. "I was so afraid I'd bore you, I went to the library the week before the dance and memorized an entire book of jokes."

"I guessed as much." He grinned knowingly. Too knowingly. "It was flattering, Kayla. You were very sweet."

She swallowed. Oh, Lord, he knew about her crush on him! Now she really was embarrassed. The waitress's appearance woke them both to the realization they'd forgotten about their food.

Matt sat back, looking at Kayla. She nodded and he told the waitress they were done.

"One thing about that dance still puzzles me," Kayla said, when the woman had left. "Why did you agree to be my escort?"

"Why? Because I was asked."

"Your father didn't pressure you?"

"Only a little, but I didn't mind. I remembered you from your visits to his office, and, well, there was something about you that had always intrigued me."

Kayla's eyebrows arched in surprise. "You're joking."

"Are you fishing for compliments, Ms. Brayton?" His smile dazzled her. The waitress came with the tab and left with Matt's credit card, all without Kayla noticing.

"To be honest," he said, his smile fading, "there's one aspect of that dance that does still bother me. I've often thought it was wrong of me to dance with you the way I did, and kiss you. Afterward I worried that you'd interpreted my actions as springing from pity."

"Didn't they?"

Matt shook his head. "Anger, Kayla. I was so angry at those jackasses we overheard, I could barely see straight. I hope you'll forgive me if I hurt or embarrassed you in any way. It was the farthest thing from my mind."

"No need to apologize." Kayla smiled softly, feeling mildly euphoric. It was amazing how differently he'd remembered that dance, and her.

He continued to watch her. "Frank is a very lucky guy, Kayla. I hope he realizes how lucky."

Her heart soared with the compliment. And then took a nosedive. Frank. The reference to him made her wilt.

Which was a ridiculous thing to have happen. Okay, so maybe she didn't feel the giddy raptures of a teenage crush when she thought of Frank, but so what? She wasn't a teenager. What better person to consider marrying than your work partner, your helpmate, your sharer of dreams? They'd make a good life together, and as her father had often said, they'd be good for Brayton's.

"No, I'm the lucky one, Matt," she murmured, but her voice lacked conviction. Although her eyes were downcast, she knew Matt was staring at her, studying her, frowning.

Finally he rose and slipped his wallet into his pocket. "Would you like to go to the square and listen to the music for a while?"

She glanced at her watch. "Sure. That sounds lovely."

The square was a broad paved area with park benches along its perimeter and a gazebo at its center where local musicians played day and night, lending the marketplace a continuously festive air. Stores and restaurants, from posh to casual, crowded in on three sides. The fourth was the waterfront. Around the gazebo, a throng of carefree vacationers was dancing to a tune with a Bahamian goombay beat. Multicolored lights had come on, rimming the bars and the bandstand.

Kayla and Matt stood on the sidelines, watching the diners and dancers, the shoppers and drinkers, while the scent of brine and bougainvillea mixed with the aroma of mouth-watering foods. Strains of a Jimmy Buffet song, drifting from one night spot, tangled with laughter and a dreamy Caribbean tune being played somewhere else on a steel drum. Kayla closed her eyes and sighed. Hard as she'd tried to fight it, she definitely felt she was on vacation now.

"Lady, would you like some braids?"

She opened her eyes to a dark, inquiring face. "No, thank you."

The woman sauntered away, hips swaying as gracefully as a palm, and Matt asked, "How many times have you been approached today?"

"At least a dozen."

"Maybe you'd save yourself some aggravation if you just gave in."

She eyed him dubiously. "I don't think so, Matthew."

The vocalist with the band in the gazebo took the microphone and announced it was time to learn the merengue, the national dance of the Bahamas. Taking a partner, he then went through the steps slowly, while the crowd filling the square followed along.

Without realizing it, Kayla began to sway, foot to foot, dipping one knee, then the other. She liked to dance, although she didn't often get the chance, and this merengue business looked relatively easy. Fun, too. People everywhere were laughing at their bumbling efforts.

"Come on. Let's try it." Matt grabbed her hand. Kayla's heart hammered. It probably wasn't a good idea for them to dance. But how could she express her trepidation without revealing her vulnerability to him, as well?

They entered the dance slowly at first, stiffly, but before long their tentativeness was gone. Soon they were moving as if they'd been partners all their lives.

Stepping right, stepping left, their lower bodies swung in time. Like pendulums, Kayla thought, smiling in delight, letting the ticktock rhythm of the island music guide her.

Stepping right, stepping left, Matt turned Kayla round so that she found herself positioned with her backside to his front. And all the while they continued to move in unison, catching every single swaying beat.

Kayla laughed to mask her self-consciousness. These steps brought bodies into fairly intimate contact. To distract herself, she pondered the mystery of why hot climates seemed to produce such sensuous dances.

But with another smooth maneuver, the thought was gone, because Matt had turned them back to back, and body parts she preferred not to think about were brushing against each other, while she and Matt continued to swing, stepping right, stepping left, to the fluid magic of the islands.

With another ticktocking turn, Matt was holding her face to face again or, as their instructor called it, belly to belly. He smiled at her, a smile straight out of her dreams, and Kayla felt a warm, melty sensation spilling deep inside her.

She began to feel caught in a warm, pink fog. Around her the colored lights blurred and the music grew muted as Matt continued to watch her. Ever so gradually, the lines of his face grew serious, and their steps slowed, slowed, slowed, until finally they were dancing to an entirely different music than everyone else in the square. Every coherent thought fled her brain, while a moment of infinite awareness opened between them.

Several seconds passed before she realized the musicians had stopped playing. Matt, too, seemed a little surprised by the silence. He released her and stepped away, wearing a small frown of confusion.

"Want to take a walk?" He cast a glance out toward the long docks.

She pulled in a deep breath, trying to shake the spell the dance had thrown over her. "It's getting late, Matt. Maybe we'd better go home and get some sleep, especially if we're planning to go snorkeling tomorrow."

He nodded. "I think it's best."

The house was dark and still when the taxi dropped them off. They tiptoed in, up the stairs and past the closed door of the room the older couple shared. From within came the peaceful sound of two people quietly snoring.

Kayla's steps slowed, an inexplicable onslaught of emotion weighing her down. Dejection, mostly. Her grandmother had hardly ever reprimanded her, and never as emphatically as she had today. Then she'd gone off with Philip, making it clear where she'd transferred her affection. Now, listening at the door to the intertwined harmony of their breathing, Kayla felt utterly shut out.

Matt nudged her arm, and with a tip of his head urged her to keep walking. She nodded, her gloom chased away by memories of all the wonderful things they'd done that day.

But at her bedroom door, they hesitated again.

"See you in the morning," she whispered.

And he replied, "Sleep well."

"I'll try."

"Me, too." His eyes locked with hers, lips slightly parted as if wanting to say more. But finally he just said good-night and walked into his room.

She was thankful he did. Had it been up to her, they would still be standing there when the sun came up the next morning.

CHAPTER SEVEN

KAYLA opened her eyes and smiled. Buttery sunlight was pouring through her open windows, bringing with it the briny scent of the sea and the soft swish of palm fronds. Her smile broadened. She was going snorkeling today.

Stretching her arms wide, she marveled at the childlike expectancy bubbling inside her. Was she developing a taste for new experiences, she, whose life had been regulated by time and routine for as long as she could remember?

She took a hasty shower, wiggled into her new bathing suit, briefly pondered her hair, decided to simply tie it at her nape with a cloth-covered elastic, pulled on her shorts and shirt and stepped into her shoes. Twelve minutes. Record time.

She found Matt sitting outside, sipping coffee and reading another outdated newspaper, same as yesterday, except that today he was wearing navy swim trunks and appeared more rested. His eyes lifted and locked with hers in a silent but eloquent greeting. She could no more look away than stop the color from blooming in her cheeks.

He wasn't wearing a shirt, and the lean musculature of his torso, dusted with just the perfect amount of dark hair, gave new meaning to the term "washboard abs". Lord, he had to be the most attractive man alive. The simple act of looking at him made her breath whoosh out of her.

Memories of the previous day returned—the easy laughter they'd shared in the casino, the torrential conversation at dinner, the dreamy exhilaration of dancing in the square—and she was forced to admit that Matthew Reed was a lot more than just a physically attractive man. Some mysterious aspect of his personality clicked with hers, turned a key, setting her free to relax and enjoy herself in a fashion she'd never experienced before.

"Good morning." His eyes held a smile that hinted he was remembering yesterday, too. But then he tilted his head, directing her attention to Ruth and Philip, who were strolling among the trees and shrubs, assiduously avoiding them. Ah, yes. Ruth. Philip. Yesterday's argument. She nodded in understanding. Matt got to his feet and together they joined the older couple.

"Morning, Gran. Philip."

Ruth sniffed at a particularly fragrant blossom. Kayla hadn't taken much notice of the garden yesterday, but now the sweet perfume of gardenias and the splashy hues of hibiscus made her wonder how she *couldn't* have been aware of it.

"Gran? Philip?" she tried again. "Can we talk?"

The older couple took their time turning their attention on her. "What about?" Ruth asked.

"I want to apologize for yesterday."

"So do I," Matt added. "If we spoke out of line it was only because we love you and are concerned about you."

"And we don't want you to be unhappy because of anything we've said."

Ruth held her head at a proud angle. "Have you changed your mind about our getting married, then?"

"To be honest, no, Gran. But we don't want to argue about it anymore." That didn't mean she wouldn't talk about it. But argue? No.

Philip caught Ruth's eye, and Kayla saw their hesitancy. They knew the truce was only temporary, the issue far from over. Still, he replied, "We can live with that."

"Great." Kayla beamed. "Now, if the invitation is still open, we'd like to go snorkeling with you today."

Ruth surrendered to a burgeoning smile. "Let's have some breakfast first and then we'll be off."

They took the eleven o'clock boat out of Port Lucaya—at eleven-thirty, of course—and within half an hour reached the coral reef where they spent the next hour exploring.

Kayla was utterly amazed, first by the fact that she *could* snorkel after just a few words of instruction, and second by the underwater realm that opened up to her as a bonus—the fancifully shaped, jewel-toned fish; the exotic plants blooming and gracefully swaying in the crystalline water; and, oh, the coral, the infinitely varied forms and colors of the coral!

She was disappointed, therefore, to see Ruth return to the boat after just twenty minutes. The woman was sitting on the broad stairs that descended from the rear deck to the water. When Kayla noticed how heavily she was breathing, her disappointment gave way to alarm.

"Anything wrong?" she called, gripping the handrail.

"Not at all. I just know my physical limitations." Ruth tugged off her right fin and smiled.

"Do you want company?"

Ruth waved her off. "No, I'm fine. I had a marvelous swim, and now I'm going to have an equally marvelous time sitting here in the sun."

She did look content, Kayla decided. After giving Ruth one last careful look, she fit her mask and snorkel in place and returned to the wondrous underwater world that was disturbed only by the rasp of her breathing.

Her heartbeat skipped when she spotted Matt swimming toward her, upward from a dive to the sandy bottom of a chasm in the reef. His dark hair fanned and swirled with his strokes. He was smiling around his mouthpiece.

Breaking through the surface, he blew the water out of his snorkel. "Follow me. I want to show you something."

They glided along on the water's surface, their masks providing a window on the world below. Occasionally their legs brushed, a feeling as diaphanous as the fins of an angelfish.

At one point Matt touched her wrist, pointed and shook his head in warning. A huge mound of mustard coral, capable of delivering a nasty burn if brushed, was growing dangerously close to the surface just ahead. Her pulse raced as she kicked extra hard to circumvent the danger.

They slipped over a garden of elk-horn coral where tiny multicolored fish darted among the sponges and slowly fanning, bright purple seaweed. Matt gestured for her to pause while he surveyed the area. She watched, wondering what he was looking for. After a while he surfaced.

"I can't find him."

"Who?"

"The stingray. He must've burrowed into the sand."

"A stingray?" Kayla gave her surroundings a slightly alarmed scan.

"Damn! I really wanted you to see him."

Although she preferred *not* to meet up with a stingray, she felt a pleasurable warmth in knowing that Matt had so wanted to share his discovery with her.

"Getting tired?" he asked.

"No. I could do this for hours."

Matt smiled, his strong, even teeth white against the bronze of his skin. In just two days he'd soaked up a remarkable tan. "I could, too. Unfortunately we only have a few more minutes."

"Then let's make the most of them."

The sun beat down so strong and clear on the return trip, Kayla could feel her bathing suit drying by the minute. She sat in her deck chair with legs and arms sprawled. Beside her, Matt lounged in a similarly relaxed fashion. She sighed contentedly, savoring the gentle rock of the boat, the warm breeze rippling through her wet hair, salt water tickling her skin as it dried. Chicago had become a distant memory.

When she accepted a Bahama Mama from one of the crew, Matt gave her leg a lethargic nudge with his knee. "You're going to get addicted to those things."

"Mind your own business, Reed," she replied, nudging him back. "I don't criticize you when you order that Bahamian beer. What's it called? Kalik?"

He lifted a tall plastic cup from under his chair and cavalierly tapped it against hers before taking a swallow. "Have I told you yet how great that suit looks on you?"

She nearly choked and sat up.

"Personally, I'm partial to bikinis," he went on, "and I didn't have much hope for that little number. But..." His eyes glinted as they flicked over her.

"But what?" she prodded shamelessly.

His strong, beautifully shaped mouth twitched. "Nice. Very nice."

Shaking her head in disparagement, she said, "Would you mind finding something else to entertain your little mind?" She took a sip of her drink and then, surrendering to some inner devil, winked at him over the rim of her cup. He laughed.

With a start Kayla realized that Ruth, standing with her back to the rail, was watching them, her gaze moving speculatively from her granddaughter to Matt.

Good Lord, she was flirting! Caught in the act, Kayla felt her temples pound. She'd become so lost in enjoying the adrenaline rush that accompanied the activity, she hadn't realized what she was doing or that she was making a spectacle of herself. What was the matter with her? What had happened to her vow not to get pulled in by this man's appeal? Where had her fear of being hurt fled? She reached for her polo shirt, yanked it over her head and hurried toward the stairs to ride out the remainder of the journey alone on the upper deck.

Back at the Lucaya marketplace, Philip suggested they try a particular restaurant for lunch, but on the way Ruth's face lit with a different idea. She herded them toward a cart where a brawny Bahamian was holding the attention of several onlookers.

"What's he doing?" Kayla craned to see better.

"He's preparing conch salad, dear. Would you like to try some?"

Kayla watched the man dredge a large conch shell from a barrel of brine, give it a few mysterious taps with a hammer and then pull out a slithery hank of meat. "Oh, I don't think so."

"It's really quite good."

Kayla had serious doubts but continued to watch, fascinated in spite of herself. The man deftly set about slicing the seafood and then dicing it until it was as fine as the tomato, green pepper and onion heaped to one side of his cutting board. He scraped all these ingredients into a bowl, squeezed the juice of a couple of limes into it, and added a touch of minced hot pepper.

Matt was watching with equal interest, standing so close to Kayla that their arms pressed. Although she seemed to be concentrating on the chef, all her awareness had fixed on that inadvertent yet electrifying contact.

"How about if I order some and you try mine before deciding?" Matt suggested. Kayla smiled at him in gratitude.

When he'd been handed his bowl, along with a bottle of Kalik, he tasted a spoonful, chewing with the attention of a gourmand. Finally he nodded his approval, and half-filling the spoon, held it out to Kayla. When she hesitated, he laughed and tried to fit the spoon between her lips, which immediately pressed tighter than a clam shell.

"You're worse than a kid taking medicine. Come on, Kayla. Really, it's very good."

"You..." All it took was that one syllable, and the spoon slid into her mouth. Kayla's eyes rounded. As far as she could see, she had two choices—to chew or spit. She chewed.

It didn't take long for the hot pepper to make itself known. She swallowed, eyes watering, and fanned her mouth. "Lend me that beer," she gasped and then snatched the bottle from Matt's hand. She'd never liked the taste of beer, but now she took a generous sip.

"Well?" Matt inquired. "What's the verdict?"

"I... like it."

"You do?"

Her smile broadened as she nodded with deeper conviction.

Matt stepped to the cart and ordered her a bowl, light on the hot pepper. It was then that Kayla noticed that she and Matt were being watched again, this time by Ruth and Philip both. She felt an urge to shout, "What? What are you looking at?" But she thought she already knew. Despite her embarrassment on the boat and her intention to proceed with decorum, she'd slipped again. She'd been drawn in by Matt's charm and become stupidly beguiled. For the past several minutes she'd forgotten the older couple, and all her attention had narrowed to Matt.

"Kayla, come with me," Ruth said when they'd finished their impromptu meal. "Let me buy you a souvenir." Without waiting, she got up from the umbrella table where they'd eaten and walked toward a cart heaped with T-shirts.

Kayla considered protesting, but truth was, she could use more clothing. She got up and followed.

They were examining the merchandise when Ruth asked, "So, what's going on between you and Matthew?"

Kayla had half expected the question. "Nothing. He's just become a good friend, somebody I can joke with." She shook out a blue shirt printed with a conch shell. "This is nice."

"It's more than friendship, Kayla. There's something..." Ruth pursed her lips, thinking. "A rapport. An intimacy. I noticed it especially when you two drank from the same bottle and ate from the same spoon. Not only was that totally unlike you, but neither of you even blinked."

Kayla felt feverish at the memory. That *had* been intimate—and so idiotically exciting she didn't know how to explain it even to herself.

"You're reading too much into it, Gran. I'm dating another man. Fairly seriously. You are aware of that fact, aren't you?"

The silence lengthened, and when Kayla looked across the table, her grandmother's face was solemn. "Yes, I am. Are you?"

Kayla swallowed. Just then a young Bahamian woman sidled up to her. "Braids, pretty lady? Would you like some braids?"

Kayla swung on her. "No! No braids." Remorse gripped her immediately. "I'm sorry. I didn't mean..." But the young woman had already walked away.

"Oh, Kayla, we do have to talk." Ruth's shrewd old eyes caught hers in a disconcerting stare.

"I'll take this one." Kayla grabbed blindly at a pink shirt embossed with a parasail and the slogan Flying Free in Freeport.

"Fine." Ruth purchased the pink shirt as well as the blue one with the conch shell. But when they should have rejoined the men, Ruth held Kayla back.

"I'm not sure if this is the right time to broach the subject, but..." Ruth paused a heartbeat. "Kayla, are you in love with Frank?"

Kayla felt her color ebb. "What kind of question is that?"

"A pretty impudent one, I suppose." Ruth chuckled. "But you have to understand, I'm your grandmother, I love you and just want the best for you, and if you're considering marriage—"

"Frank *is* the best. He's a wonderful man." Kayla plucked a leathery leaf from an overhanging vine and pulled it apart again and again.

"I know he's wonderful. He's good-looking and intelligent and, after Gordon, he's your father's favorite golden boy. But I was thinking, Kayla, what if Brayton's didn't exist? Do you think you'd still be involved with him? Without the clockworks, would you two still be considering marriage?"

Kayla flung the shredded leaf. "But Brayton's does exist."

"Why are you so upset?"

"I'm not upset."

"Kayla, you're snapping worse than a flag in a gale. And you're trembling."

Kayla closed her eyes and took a deep breath. "I'm sorry." How had the focus of this visit got so turned around? Why were they standing here discussing her and Frank when the problem of Ruth and Philip still needed resolving?

Just then Philip called that he and Matt were going into a nearby museum shop that displayed old pirate coins and bottles.

Left with Ruth, Kayla saw no easy exit from the conversation. "I'm upset because you seem to be implying there's something between me and Matt, and honestly there isn't. We have nothing in common. I don't understand the first thing about commodities, and he couldn't care less about German clock movements. Oh, and have I mentioned we live a thousand miles apart?"

Ruth eyed her calmly. "Seems you've given the relationship some thought."

"There *is* no relationship. I'm sorry if that spoils some fantasy you've harbored since I was a girl..."

"Oh, I gave that up long ago. I can't deny that I did think you'd make a nice pair, once upon a time. But after that date I arranged, when you came home so quiet and he never called again..." Ruth shrugged, a lift of shoulders and palms that conveyed her acceptance that she'd made a mistake. "My only defense is, I knew you were in love with him, and—"

"Teenagers have crushes, Gran. Crushes, that's all."

"Whatever. I just wanted to give you a chance with him, and if it didn't work out, well, at least you'd have one night to remember."

Oh, she'd remembered, all right. Every humiliating detail.

"But that's neither here nor there now." Ruth squared her shoulders, eager to make a point. But then she frowned. "What were we talking about?"

Kayla waited. Surely Ruth would remember—Frank, her relationship with him—but she waited in vain.

"Honestly, sometimes I think I'd lose my head if it weren't screwed on."

"It wasn't important, Gran."

"Oh, I remember. Matthew."

Kayla groaned. "Why do you keep insisting I get involved with him?"

"I don't. That's my point. I'm not sure it's wise."

"Oh." Kayla's jangled nerves went strangely quiet at this turnabout.

"You realize he's been married, don't you?"

"Yes, he told me."

"He was really hurt, Kayla. Too hurt, Phil sometimes thinks. Since his divorce, he's made a career out of avoiding serious involvement."

"He told me he needs to focus on his work."

"Maybe, but Phil thinks he's really just afraid of being hurt again. His work has become a cover. He uses it so he won't have to get out there and risk falling in love again. Not that he doesn't see women. He does, quite a few. But that's just another symptom of his problem. He sees too many to get serious with anyone."

Kayla fixed her gaze on a small lizard dozing in a flower border. "Is that what Phil meant the other night when he made that strange comment about being thankful he was still emotionally vulnerable? When he implied that Matt wasn't?"

"Yes. Phil's afraid that, without realizing it, Matt has so hardened himself to love that he's become impervious to it."

"Do you agree?"

"I'm not sure. The way he's been looking at you—"

"Oh, Gran! I told you it's nothing."

"You're probably right. And that's precisely why I felt I should warn you."

"Thanks, I appreciate your concern, but I really don't need to be warned. I'm not about to let myself become anyone's vacation dalliance."

"Good." Ruth gave Kayla's arm a squeeze. "Let's go join the men."

Kayla wandered through the coin museum in a fog. Matt asked if she was all right and she said she was, but when she looked into his perplexed gray eyes, her insides clenched with something akin to grief. Which was ridiculous, of course. Did his private life really concern her? In a couple of days they'd be leaving here, never to see each other again. Whether or not his wife had hurt him, whether or not he was soured on love, didn't matter. Actually it just reinforced the other reasons she had for not getting involved with him.

With an effort, she banished her gloom and put on a smile. If she had only a couple of days left here, she refused to let things that didn't concern her get her down.

They finished visiting the museum and were on their way to a ticket agency to see about a dinner cruise when Philip and Ruth stepped aside and began talking in hushed tones.

"Hey, folks," Philip called. "Ruthie and I are going to head back to the house."

"Are you all right, Ruth?" Matt asked.

"Just a little tired. I've become used to taking a nap in the afternoon."

"Her stomach's upset, too."

"It's just a touch of indigestion, Phil. Those onions in the conch salad."

Kayla frowned. "Are you sure you're all right?"

"Positive. You two stay and enjoy yourselves. We'll see you—" she wafted a hand "—whenever."

Matt and Kayla did remain at the marketplace, but after having spent the previous day at the international bazaar, they weren't in much of a mood to shop again. When Kayla mentioned offhandedly that she wished she were still snorkeling, Matt didn't hesitate to haul her down to the dock, where they took the last boat of the day out to the reef.

They returned to the house in the early evening exhilarated but feeling slightly guilty for having gone to dinner without the older couple. Oddly the door was locked and no one answered when Matt rang the bell. Using their key, they let themselves in and found that the drapes, drawn during the hot afternoon, hadn't been opened yet. Kayla's skin crawled with foreboding.

"Gran?" she called, peering out the back window. The moon was rising languidly over the ocean in a lavender sky.

"There's a note on the dining room table," Matt called.

From the firm set of his mouth when he handed it to her, she knew the message wasn't good.

"Matt, Kayla," Philip had scrawled in uncharacteristic haste. "It's now five o'clock and Ruth still isn't feeling well, so I think it's best we have this indigestion checked out. Going to the hospital. Don't get alarmed. We'll probably be back before you even read this."

The paper shook as Kayla lowered it to the table. She wasn't that knowledgeable about the symptoms of an impending heart attack, but she did know that a feeling similar to indigestion could be one of them. "What t-time is it?" she stammered.

"Seven-thirty."

Which meant her grandmother might've been lying in some strange ICU for the past two hours, not knowing anyone, not familiar to any of the doctors or nurses attending her. A wave of panic seemed to drain all her strength.

"Damn. I bet our taxi already left." Matt sped to the front door.

"Never mind. I'll call another."

Kayla had her hand on the phone when she heard Matt holler and whistle. Apparently the taxi was still within hailing distance. "Come on. We've got our ride," he said.

CHAPTER EIGHT

THEY found Ruth in an examining room in emergency. She was sitting up in a chair wearing a hospital gown and a thoroughly put-upon expression. Philip sat beside her, holding her hand.

"Oh, Gran!" Kayla rushed to her. "Are you all right? I'm sorry I stayed out so late. What happened? Have you seen a doctor yet?" She squatted in front of the old woman, gripping the hand that Philip wasn't holding.

Ruth chuckled. "The first thing you can do is calm down, love. I have no intention of croaking just yet. The second thing is, decide which question you want me to answer first."

"Are you in any discomfort?" Kayla asked, realizing it was yet another question.

"A little, but it's mostly gastric."

Kayla felt the warmth of Matt's body behind her, his hands resting on her shoulders.

"That right, Dad?" he asked.

Philip raised his eyes. It was then that Kayla noticed how bloodshot they were, how drawn and pale was his face. "The doctor who examined her says she's probably right, but he ran the usual tests anyway, just to be sure."

"At your insistence," Ruth reminded him in exasperation. But it was a feigned exasperation. There was no missing the warmth that lit her eyes as she gazed at Philip.

He said, "We're waiting for the results of the EKG now."

"Have a seat, you two," Ruth suggested.

Matt pulled forward a chair for Kayla but remained standing himself.

Ruth chuckled. "Kayla Marie Brayton, I don't believe you entered a public building looking like that."

Kayla glanced down at her rumpled shorts and shirt, smeared with catsup from dinner. Damp patches testified to the itchy fact that her bathing suit still hadn't completely dried, and her hair, dull from salt water, hung in a messy ponytail.

She smiled faintly. "For some bizarre reason, I don't care, Gran. Being here with you is all that matters."

Just then a short, heavyset doctor with woolly gray hair entered the room, a thick folder clutched to the front of his white lab coat. Kayla was still holding Ruth's hand and felt the old woman's pulse leap. Evidently Ruth wasn't as calm or unconcerned about her condition as she appeared.

"Ah, I see you have company, Mrs. Brayton," the doctor said.

Ruth introduced them.

"How do you do?" He shook Kayla's hand, then Matt's. When he opened Ruth's folder, Kayla gaped at the large amount of paperwork the hospital had compiled on her in so short a time. It did nothing to ease her sense of alarm.

"Well?" Ruth inquired, stoically lifting her chin.

"You're fine, Mrs. Brayton. I can't find any evidence of unusual coronary activity."

Ruth let out a soft cry. Flooded with relief, Kayla moved to embrace her, but found she was already in someone else's arms—Philip's. His eyes were closed, his face muscles tight, and moisture glistened along his thin lashes.

Kayla eased away from them, heavy with dejection, even while part of her was still rejoicing at the good news. She wasn't needed here. Ruth had turned to Philip instinctively.

Again Matt's strong hands closed over her shoulders. She sighed, sagging against him, grateful he was there. She sensed he understood her ambivalent feelings—and maybe more than she cared to dwell on.

"In fact," the physician continued, "from the records you provided, I'd say you're in remarkably good health, Mrs. Brayton. You've made outstanding progress since your episode last August."

Ruth had brought her medical records? Kayla sat up straighter, trying to see into the folder.

The doctor shuffled through the reports, discussing Ruth's program of rehabilitation, searching for something innovative in her treatment. But he found nothing new, nothing he wouldn't have prescribed himself.

"Why, it's simple, Doctor." Ruth's smile lit her whole face. "Love. That's what's helped me get better so fast."

Kayla shifted with mild embarrassment, but surprisingly the doctor didn't contradict her grandmother. "That could very well be," he said. "I've had patients get over the darnedest things with the help of positive thinking, and what's more positive than being in love, eh?" His eyes twinkled merrily.

"Am I free to go, then?"

"Yes, ma'am. I recommend you stop at a drugstore to pick up an antacid or bicarbonate of soda. A warm towel or hot-water bottle pressed to the stomach often brings relief, too. And in the future, avoid spicy foods, okay?"

Ruth pouted sulkily.

"I know, I know," the affable physician commiserated. "Life isn't fair. With me, it's tomato sauce, any kind. And I love Italian food."

Later that night, after Ruth was comfortably tucked into bed, Philip joined Matt and Kayla on the patio with one of his thin cigars. The men talked quietly at the table while Kayla reclined on a nearby chaise, deep in thought.

"Philip, can you tell me something?" she finally asked. "My grandmother's heart attack—was it stress-induced?"

"Most definitely. In combination with somewhat restricted arteries. She never slowed down, Kayla. She was working and worrying as hard at seventy-one as she used to at forty-one."

Kayla sighed and pondered the bright canopy of stars. Had she created more stress in her grandmother's life with this visit? Had she tired Ruth out? Induced indigestion with her opposition to the marriage? Lord, how much time human beings wasted making other human beings unhappy.

Phil raised his cigar and studied its glowing tip. "But then, I'm hardly the person to criticize anybody's work habits. After my wife's death I myself almost had a stroke. Ah, the good old American work cure." He shook his head and glanced meaningfully at his son.

"You look tired, Dad," Matt said.

Philip shrugged dismissively, but his son was right, and he admitted as much by hauling himself to his feet. "If you two don't mind, I think I will turn in."

"Good night, Philip," Kayla said. Then, swallowing her pride, she added, "And thank you."

"For what?" Already shuffling toward the house, he clearly expected no answer.

"For insisting Ruth go to the hospital. For making sure she traveled with her medical records. For worrying and taking such good care of her. I know it can't be easy."

Philip paused, struck by Kayla's capitulation. "There you're wrong, sweetheart. When you love somebody, it's the easiest thing in the world. Good night."

When he was gone, Matt came to sit with Kayla on the chaise. It was double-wide and accommodated them with ease. After the scare Ruth had put her through, she welcomed his company, welcomed his calm strength and the sense of comradeship that came from having weathered the scare with him.

"How're you doing?" he asked softly.

"Not great." She sighed, which caused their arms to brush—silky, sun-drenched skin against hard, hair-coarsened muscle. It was comforting, this making contact with another human being, and she didn't even try to move away. "It isn't easy being so confused."

"What confuses you?"

"Ruth. Philip. My accusation that he's only after her money."

Matt nodded. "I feel pretty much the same about my accusation that she's just using him to escape your father's control." He moved and she became aware of soft denim meeting her bare leg.

"He was genuinely worried about her today, Matt."

"I know. And when she got the news that she was all right, she turned to him so automatically." He sighed heavily. "Maybe we're not confused, Kayla, just having trouble swallowing our humble pie."

She smiled faintly. "Could be."

Matt's long left foot, bare, angled under her smaller right one, also bare. Again, contact felt comforting. Too comforting. For a moment her thoughts became so scrambled she couldn't speak.

"I have a question." Matt nudged her foot with his toes.

"What?" The word came out shuddery and breathless. Good Lord, this wasn't just companionship she was feeling. Maybe it had started out as such, but it wasn't anymore.

"Are you beginning to cave in regarding their plans to be married?"

Kayla turned her head to look at him. He did the same. When their eyes met, she experienced that all too familiar sensation of tumbling down an elevator shaft. But the strange thing about it tonight was, she didn't care. Too tired to fight it, she let herself tumble away. "Are you?" she asked.

"I'm not sure." In the moonlight his mouth became more intriguing than any mystery, his eyes deeper than any sky. Too softly he asked, "Have you seen the way they look at each other?"

She swallowed, thinking the way she was looking at him was probably a good imitation. "I'm really confused."

"That makes two of us." He took her hand and she didn't pull away. His touch felt too good, those strong fingers wrapped around hers, that broad thumb stroking her knuckles. She'd read somewhere that a wide thumb indicated a sensuous nature, but she didn't need a magazine article to tell her that. She'd seen how he enjoyed music and good food. She'd watched him savor the sun on his back, admire the colors in a seashell, and, oh, how he loved to touch. He was always touching her, she'd noticed.

How different he was from Frank. She'd never put Frank on a sensuality scale before, but now that she was sharing her time and quarters with someone with whom she could compare him, she realized Frank came out a lightweight.

Not that it really mattered. She and Frank had other things going for them. Lots of other things.

Still, she couldn't help feeling cheated, robbed of all the nights in her future that could, but wouldn't, be spent lying in a chaise under the stars with someone she adored to distraction.

The thought caught her like a physical blow. Adored to distraction?

Matt Reed was a very attractive man, a compelling and virile man. It was only natural for her to react to him on some feminine, sexual level. But that didn't mean she *adored* him. It didn't mean anything except that she was a normal, healthy woman.

So, what *did* this feeling of being cheated mean? That she didn't adore Frank to distraction? She already knew that and had accepted that it didn't matter.

Or had she? Was the snappishness she'd exhibited, when Ruth asked if she loved Frank, a sign that she had not accepted the fact? That she was, in reality, upset by it?

She was gnawing on her lip when Matt whispered huskily, "A penny for your thoughts."

She searched for a topic safer than the one that was actually consuming her. She latched onto the first thing that came to mind. "I've been thinking about my grandmother's new philosophy, that carpe diem business. I'm reluctant to say this, Matt, but I'm beginning to understand what she meant. While we were racing off to the hospital, not knowing what condition we'd find her in, I kept hearing her words, you know, about life not being a dress rehearsal? It was such an odd sensation, such a direct perception of the shortness of life."

Matt grunted. "I experienced something similar when we got to the hospital. Looking at my father, I began to see things through his eyes. I swear, for a while I even felt his anguish as if I were inside his skin."

"Yes!" It pleased her inordinately that Matt understood the elusive experience she was trying to express. "It wasn't so much a *thinking* about their situation as a *feeling* it."

"It kills me to admit this," Matt added, "but while we were at the hospital I even began to think that maybe it doesn't matter if Ruth serves as an emotional Band-Aid to help my father deal with my mother's death."

Kayla sighed. "And maybe it doesn't matter that Philip provides my grandmother with an escape from my father and the realities of aging. For whatever reasons, they love each other and are there for each other."

Matt lifted her hand, rocking it rhythmically from the elbow, like a sleepy arm wrestler. "The present moment, that's really all they've got, isn't it? The past is past, the future uncertain. And it's pretty damned arrogant of us to think we have the right to stop them."

"From—" she gulped "—getting married?"

"Mmm." He rocked her hand one last time before guiding it down to the valley between them where her knuckles pressed his thigh and his pressed hers. She shivered and he asked, "Cold?"

"No, just wondering how the *devil* I'm going to tell my father."

Matt sat quiet and motionless a long while. Finally he asked, "Do you always worry so much about what your father will say?"

She opened her mouth to object, then shut it with a surprised snap. She did worry. Always had. But no one had ever noticed before, or called her on it.

"His approval seems to mean a lot to you."

"Well, of course. Everyone enjoys the approval of their parents."

Matt got to his feet and lowered the back of the chaise. "Sure," he agreed, returning and lying on his side so that he faced her more directly. "But with you it's different. It's a need, Kayla, one that eats away at you." He breathed out an unthinking laugh. "Jeez, what did Lloyd do to you when you were a kid, anyway? Blame you for your mother's death?"

Kayla didn't so much as blink, yet she felt stricken. Lying stiff and flat, she fixed her gaze on the night sky and concentrated on fighting the burning in her eyes. It was a losing battle, however, and soon the stars swam and blurred.

"Kayla?" Matt braced himself on one elbow. "Hey, what's going on?" He cupped her cheek and forced her to turn her head. She lowered her eyes, but a tear trickled over the bridge of her nose, anyway.

"Oh, hell!" he muttered. "I didn't mean—I'm sorry. I was only— The thought of any parent doing such a thing seemed so cruel and remote, I really didn't expect—"

"Shh. It's okay. My father has never actually said the words. It's just a feeling I've picked up over the years. I don't know why—except that nothing I do seems to please him, as opposed to Gordon, who can do no wrong." She smiled feebly and shrugged. "Maybe I just imagined it. My brother *is* smarter than I am. It was only natural for me to grow up feeling I didn't measure up. Happens all the time between siblings."

Matt smoothed her hair, stroking her with a tenderness that was almost her undoing. "Is that why you've spent the past five years living in five different cities, knocking yourself out to build up the retail chain? To do something Gordon hasn't done? To impress your father?"

She was about to say no, was already shaking her head, when suddenly she paused. Veils seemed to lift from her eyes, revealing an aspect of herself that she'd never noticed before.

"Turn to me, Kayla. Look at me," Matt urged in a quiet but compelling voice.

Still somewhat dazed by her moment of self-awareness, she turned on her side and tucked her fist under her cheek.

"Well?" he asked.

Her pulse accelerated. She didn't particularly like what she'd learned about herself. Yet Matt made her feel at ease, trusting, as if she could admit anything to him and it would be okay. "Yes, I think you're right," she conceded softly. And, falling deeper into the safety net of his eyes, she whispered, "Yes," again.

For a long while they lay without speaking, eye to eye, nose to nose, heart to heart.

"Tell me about it," Matt said in a husky whisper.

The night shimmered with moonlight and the lure of intimacy. Feelings suppressed too long clamored for release, but Kayla only shook her head. "Nothing to tell, really." She was afraid, if she got going, she'd come off an unattractive bundle of whining complaints.

"I don't believe that for a minute." His stare intensified. "You'd rather be back in Boston, wouldn't you?"

Kayla lowered her gaze to the dark tuft of chest hair at the V of his open-collared shirt, hoping he hadn't seen how close to the mark he'd hit again. "Not really."

"No? Then why are you still registered to vote there? Why still subscribe to *The Globe* and *The Bostonian?*"

"I don't—"

"Yes, you do. I've seen them in your briefcase."

She placed a finger over Matt's lips. "I'd rather not discuss it." He inhaled as if to speak. "Please?" she implored.

He subsided, and she was relieved. No need to get into how much she disliked continually moving. No need to divulge how hard she worked to keep her stores in the black, or how deep was her disappointment that her father had never visited them. All Lloyd knew of her efforts was what he read on her financial reports, which, after rent, utilities and salaries were paid, showed a profit of only twenty percent as opposed to the forty percent Brayton's cleared on its wholesale orders. In other words, in spite of the fact that her stores were elegant little showpieces, and twenty percent was a very satisfactory profit margin, given the poor economy, to him she was a failure. No, there was no need to get into any of that at all.

She sighed and seemed to awaken to a dreamy realization that her finger still lay on Matt's mouth. It had slid downward, though, catching on his lower lip. Bemused, she stared at that mouth, at the space between his slightly parted lips, at the faint glint of teeth, and suddenly the focus of her thoughts shifted. *He has the most beautiful mouth I've ever beheld,* she thought. And then, *The most beautiful skin. The most beautiful hair.*

Her eyes, alight with admiration, eventually met his, and when she should have looked away, she didn't. But neither did he, and in that breathless moment she knew that this fascination she was feeling was not a one-sided thing. Recklessly they each studied the other, acknowledging their mutual interest, brazenly enjoying the forbidden attraction. Sense memories of yesterday's kiss played through her body, setting off small crashes of heat, here, there, crashes that seemed to reverberate in Matt's pounding heart.

They were playing with fire. She knew it, he knew it. It was totally inappropriate that they should be lying here, weaving themselves into each other's lives. She was dating a wonderful man, a man who didn't deserve this sort of behavior from her. And he was a confirmed single, wed to his work and disillusioned with love. If they were going to save whatever honor still existed between them, now was the time. Very carefully they eased away from each other onto their backs.

"It's getting late, Matt," she murmured.

"Uh-huh," he agreed.

But neither of them moved. She lay still, afraid that if they did move, they'd touch.

"Before you go, though, before we drop what we were saying..." Matt lay a finger on the back of her wrist, the merest of touches, yet she felt fused to him at that glorious point of contact.

"Yes?" she whispered, fighting for breath.

"I really think you ought to live your own life, Kayla, not the one you think will impress your father."

She felt slightly deflated. Had she expected him to say something else?

"Your grandmother is right, you know. This isn't a dress rehearsal. This is the only life you're going to get, and maybe the time has come for you to take control of it and break free. It won't be easy, but I think the risk is worth taking. Otherwise you may never be truly happy." He sat up, dropping his feet to the tiles and his elbows to his knees. For a long while they said nothing, just listened to the swishing of the palms and the thudding of their hearts.

Finally he turned with every indication he was about to say good-night, and caught her in the act of watching him, the strong curve of his back, the breeze lifting his hair off his wide, intelligent brow. He stilled, while their eyes locked and resumed the communication they'd been engaged in earlier, the silent dialogue of mutual fascination and rising body heat.

I should go in, Kayla thought, but she could no sooner turn from his mesmerizing gaze than turn back a tide. And the next moment she was thinking, *I wish he'd kiss me.* Why didn't he? Why didn't he just give in and do it? *Kiss me, please!*

The air between them quivered with attraction, with longing. And with control. Matt swallowed hard and dragged his gaze from hers.

No, they wouldn't kiss. Couldn't kiss. Not now. Something between them had changed. Yesterday she'd been able to rationalize his affection in the bazaar by saying it was just a gesture of friendship. But the passion smoldering in his eyes just now had been much too real to dismiss.

So was the fact that he had stronger scruples.

Shame overwhelmed her. She was dating Frank and yet was throwing herself at Matt, flirting, touching, cuddling under the stars. What sort of unconscionable creature was she?

She got to her feet, angry, sad, frustrated, confused. "I'm going in, Matt. I'm bushed."

He nodded. "Me, too." But he didn't get up and follow, and when she looked out her window half an hour later, he was still sitting on the chaise, bathed in Bahama moonlight and lost in his thoughts.

CHAPTER NINE

KAYLA tossed most of that night, caught in a web of fractured conversation and skittering images.

Take control, Matt had said. Break free. But how?

The retail enterprise she was engaged in had grown far beyond anything she had anticipated at the age of twenty-two. It had become a vast and complicated machine, and she felt ensnared in its gears, inextricably so, because she was the driving force. She wasn't even sure she should want to break free. It was, after all, her life, and an enviable one by lots of people's standards.

But why was she agonizing over her career? she wondered, as her bedside clock ticked on. Matt's suggestion to take control had come on the heels of their discussion about Ruth's marrying Philip and Kayla's trepidation over phoning her father. Matt had been referring to her standing up for Ruth's right to marry whomever she pleased, that was all. Right?

So why did her life suddenly feel shaky right to its foundation?

And how *was* she going to tell her father? she thought, in the wee dark hours when the smallest doubt can grow to monstrous dimensions. What if Lloyd was right and Ruth really was placing Brayton's in jeopardy? What if Philip and Matt were the best actors on God's green earth and the family was about to lose everything it had ever worked for?

Finally sleep did claim her, but dawn arrived too soon. When she came downstairs, she had circles under her eyes and the urge to kill in her heart. She tried to say it

131

was just one of those inexplicable devil moods that possesses a person once in a blue moon, but she knew better. The mood had a source, and its name was Matt Reed.

No one was on the patio or in the garden, but the gate lay open wide. She plucked an orange off the breakfast table and headed in that direction.

She found Matt lying on the beach, face down, half his body sprawled on a short towel, the rest on the sand. When her shadow crossed his back, he opened one bleary eye, closed it, opened it, then surrendered to sleep again.

He looked as bedraggled as she felt, and yet her heart turned over just at the sight of him. Damn him. *Damn!* What was he doing to her, putting her emotions into such a spin?

On a wave of confused vexation, she kicked a spray of sand over his legs. Well, she'd *aimed* for his legs.

He shot up, spluttering and scrubbing at his face. "What the hell?"

Her expression buckled with contrition. But she didn't apologize. Perhaps if she feigned innocence, she could start over on a more civil footing. "Morning. Where is everyone?"

He brushed the fine sand from his neck and cautiously squinted up at her. "Gone for their morning walk."

"How's my grandmother feeling today?"

"Better." He shook out his towel and spread it so they both could sit. "Kayla, before they get back we've got to talk."

"About what?" She remained standing.

"A couple of things. First, Ruth and my father have decided to take a trip to Nassau after they're married, and they've asked if we'll stay here to watch over the house."

Kayla's breathing quickened. "Alone?"

"Yes. It's only an overnight trip."

She was already shaking her head. "I can't. I won't."

"Kayla, if we don't stay, they won't go, and they really, really want to go. The second thing I want to tell you is, I told Ruth and my father I'd be their best man."

Now her breathing really came short, and a pressure, like thickening steam, filled her head.

"Of course," he added, "you're free to make your own decision, but I thought you'd want to know about mine before you ran into them." His eyes narrowed. "What's the matter?"

"Nothing," she snapped.

He gripped her left ankle and tugged. With a yelp, she tumbled to the sand beside him. Her orange bounced away.

"Damn you. All right! Maybe I am upset."

"At me?"

She found her orange, rubbed the sand off and set to peeling it. "Maybe. I don't appreciate the corner you've backed me into."

"What corner?"

She cast him a don't-play-dumb look. "Your oh-so-magnanimous agreement to be their best man."

"That has nothing to do with you."

"Hell it doesn't. Do you know how inconsiderate I'll look to them if I don't follow your lead?"

"Wait a minute. Last night, didn't you agree that we have no right to oppose them? Wasn't it you who said the trip to the hospital changed your outlook?"

Her lips compressed in frustration, mostly at herself.

"Have you changed your mind?"

Still she didn't answer.

"Ah, I get it. You want to agree and be their maid of honor, but you don't want to take responsibility for your decision. You want to blame me, say I put you in a corner. Well, I've got a flash for you, kid. I'm not playing that game."

Her stomach clenched. "This isn't a game!"

"Oh, no? Come on, Kayla, grow up. Take responsibility for your choices."

"Give me a break," she drawled, her gaze sliding away in disdain. At least she hoped it looked like disdain. He'd cut to a part of her that hurt. "Aw, shoot. Here they come." She pasted on a smile. "Good morning, Gran, Philip. How are you feeling today?"

"Fit as can be. But if you don't mind, Phil and I are going to stay home today. We have some last-minute arrangements to make regarding our wedding, and, quite frankly, we'd just prefer to spend the day relaxing."

"But don't let us stop you from gallivanting," Philip added.

"Relaxing here sounds fine," Matt agreed, falling back heavily on his elbows.

"Has Matthew told you?" Ruth asked excitedly. "He's agreed to be our best man."

Kayla finished peeling her orange and tossed the rind to a pair of watchful sea gulls who immediately gobbled it up. "Yes."

Everyone looked at the gulls with rapt attention, but Kayla knew what they were thinking—and waiting for. Her heart beat faster. When the tension was finally too thick to breathe, she threw up her hands. "All right, I'll do it. I'll be your maid of honor."

"Are you still mad?" Matt asked later that morning, driving Kayla into downtown Freeport. "Have you changed your mind? And if so, why am I driving you into town to shop for a dress?"

"No, I haven't changed my mind," she admitted. But he was right about her lingering bad mood. "Watch where you're going."

Cursing, Matt swerved away from an oncoming car.

"Don't swear at me," she said. "It's not my fault you can't remember they drive on the left side of the road here."

His fists tightened around the steering wheel, muscles jumped along his jaw, and Kayla realized she *wanted* to antagonize him, *wanted* to offend. The urge pushed at her like a bully.

Apparently she was succeeding. "Look, I'm not your problem, Kayla, so get off my back." They'd reached the downtown area, and without regard to whether or not they were anywhere near a dress shop, Matt veered to the curb.

Kayla steadied herself against the dash. "Implying what? That somebody else *is?*"

"Bingo." He switched off the engine. "And I don't exactly enjoy being the target for your anger, or fear, or whatever the hell it is you feel whenever you think about calling him."

Her nerves felt stripped and raw. "Stop it. I've had about all I can take of your dime-store psychology."

Matt sank his fingers in his hair and dropped his elbows to the steering wheel. "My what?"

"You heard me. A lot of things got said last night that don't make sense today. All that stuff about taking control of my life and breaking free, for instance. From what, Matt? I've lived in six exciting cities, I'm a successful businesswoman, I'm involved in a mature relationship. How much more independent do you want me to get?"

He slowly turned his head and pinned her with a look she couldn't hold.

"Listen," she said, "all I'm saying is, I don't like your attempts to slot me after just four short days and—"

"Oh, they've been anything but short, sweetheart."

"And you can't cram all my problems into a neat compartment marked Need to Please Father."

"At least you admit you do have problems."

"So I'd appreciate it if you'd mind your own business and—"

"You're scared. You want to take charge of your life, but you don't know how. You feel stuck and you're scared."

She swallowed convulsively. "Didn't I just ask you to mind your own business? I don't poke into yours."

"Oh, I'm sure you would if you found a foothold."

He looked so arrogant she couldn't help saying, "You don't think I've seen the cracks?"

"What cracks?"

"In your facade."

"In my facade?" he mocked with drawling sarcasm.

"That's right. You're not perfect, y'know. You have hang-ups too."

Although his expression didn't change, she felt she'd caught his attention on a new level. "If you're referring to my mother's death—"

"I'm referring to your marriage, Mr. Eligible Bachelor."

He went very still. "What about my marriage?" he asked in a suddenly cold and precise voice. Just as suddenly it seemed a very bad idea to pursue this particular topic.

"Let's drop it, okay?" She reached for the door handle.

He grabbed her arm. "What about my marriage?" Her lungs felt constricted. "Well, sometimes I get the feeling—" her voice croaked "—that you haven't quite gotten over the fact that it...it failed."

Into the ensuing silence he dropped an icy, "Go on."

"What, go on? There's nothing else."

He didn't believe that any more than she'd meant it. "What's the connection with my being—" here he mimicked her sarcasm "—an eligible bachelor."

She hated the way he was goading her, hated the ice in his eyes. She searched for phrasing that would temper her meaning. "Failure stinks, Matt. And it hurts. It's only natural to become wary of relationships, and where better to hide than behind the attitude of the carefree bachelor too busy with his career to get serious?"

"Is that right?"

She nodded, but she'd lost most of her intensity. She'd wanted to strike and vex, but she'd also wanted to probe, to test the ideas Ruth had shared with her yesterday about him. Only now, looking into his haunted eyes, did she realize the depth and complexity of the wound she'd opened.

The silence spun out, tautening the atmosphere in the car until it fairly crackled. Unable to look at him she finally asked, "Aren't you going to say anything?"

In a voice so low and calm it chilled her he said, "Yes. Get out."

"What?"

"Go do your shopping."

"Are you leaving me here?" She seemed to be inhaling her words.

He kept his eyes trained on a shop window. "I'll meet you here in an hour." With no further elaboration, he got out of the car, slammed the door and stalked down the heat-shimmering sidewalk.

They rode home in prickly silence and spent the rest of the day avidly avoiding each other. Kayla worked in her room for an hour while he read on the patio, and when he moved upstairs, she moved down. From the front yard to the back, from the patio to the beach, they hopped around the property like checkers on a game board, glowering their animosity whenever they happened to cross paths.

It was exhausting work. After a swim, Kayla belly flopped onto her beach towel and within minutes fell asleep.

She awoke restive, uneasy with her body from dreams of... of what? Heat? The back of her knees felt burned. Dreams of the sun, then? The sun sliding phantom fingers along the length of her legs? Streaming phantom kisses down her back?

Kayla sat up, dizzy and fogged with sleep that swirled and spiraled but eventually parted, leaving her sickened with the vision it disclosed. Maybe it *was* the sun's heat that had penetrated her dreams and dictated their content, but that heat had taken on human form.

She turned her scowling gaze up the beach to where Matt sat under a palm tree reading a novel he'd bought in town. "Damn him to hell," she muttered, getting to her feet and wobbling to the water. If a plume of steam had hissed when she submerged, she wouldn't have been in the least surprised.

The devil mood Kayla had awakened in on Wednesday was greatly subdued by the time the sun rose on Thursday. It was Ruth's and Philip's wedding day, after all, and the least she could do was be civil to Matt in their presence.

He seemed to have come to the same conclusion. But it was a sullen civility. As they shared the breakfast table, their eyes rarely met and their words to each other were mumbled. Kayla hated the strain. After spending three delightful days with him, enjoying end-to-end chatter and activity, this distance hurt. She was sorry she'd pecked at him with such unrelenting antagonism. She didn't even know why she'd done it anymore. Today the reasons seemed so murky. She only knew she was sorry. Their time together on the island was rapidly running out, and she'd wasted an entire day.

After breakfast she offered to help her grandmother dress. Ruth was delighted with the offer.

With Ruth seated at the dressing table in her bedroom, Kayla blow-dried her freshly shampooed hair, experimenting with a small round styling brush as she worked.

"All the fuss." Ruth clucked and shook her head.

"No fuss at all. A lady deserves to look her best on her wedding day." Watching her grandmother's reflection in the mirror, she was struck by the radiant happiness shining in Ruth's eyes. Kayla's hands stilled on the old woman's head. Beneath her fingers beat a warm and steady pulse.

Reverently Kayla lowered a kiss to her grandmother's curls, her heart overflowing with love and gratitude for all the years this woman had spent mothering her. What a legacy of values she'd imparted, a legacy Ruth was apparently still working at, because the warmth beating under Kayla's fingers, the brightness in those old eyes, seemed to be whispering a lesson about life, the forward-moving, ever hopeful thrust of life—at any age.

"There, that should hold the set right through your flight to Nassau." Kayla put down the can of hair spray.

"Thank you, dear. Just help me zip up, then you can run off and get yourself ready."

Kayla removed the hanger from the ivory dress Ruth had bought at Lord & Taylor's before coming here.

"I hope you don't mind this little trip. We'll be back tomorrow night."

"What's to mind? It's your honeymoon."

"You and Matthew *will* be good children while we're gone, won't you?" Ruth said in mock reproach. Evidently she'd noticed they weren't getting along.

"Turn," Kayla said, ignoring the remark. "The only thing I don't understand is why you insist I stick around till you get back." She zipped up the dress, then held up the matching short-sleeved jacket.

"Maybe it's time I explained, then." Ruth slipped on the jacket and tugged the lapels over her bosom. "I've been doing a lot of thinking about your predicament, Kayla. Namely, the difficult task you face going back to Boston and telling your father I've married Phil. Not only that, that you were my maid of honor. So I've decided to go back with you and help break the news."

"Oh, Gran, you don't have to do that."

"But I want to. I should. This predicament is really all my doing. Besides, I've decided to put your father out of his misery and sign over my position at Brayton's to him while I'm there."

Kayla snapped to attention. "Are you sure?"

"Yes. I'm tired of the factory, Kayla. If Lloyd wants it, he's welcome to it."

"What about your vacation? You have another week here."

"I'll return just as soon as my errand in Boston is completed."

Kayla took a long, deep breath, nagged by the fact that it was the easiest breath she'd taken all week. "Fine. I'll make plane reservations for us for Saturday."

The marriage ceremony was celebrated at the Garden of the Groves, a twelve-acre botanical paradise named after the founders of Freeport, Georgette and Wallace Groves.

It was a simple ceremony conducted by a local official and witnessed by a small gathering of visitors to the garden who were delighted by the unexpected added attraction to their tour. There was no Mendelssohn March hammered out on a thundering organ, no stained glass or blaze of candles. So simple, yet Kayla was moved to tears by the beauty of it.

As she was standing by her grandmother's side, her senses seemed overloaded. The air was deliciously warm and moist, and graced with the perfume of exotic flowers and the trilling of strange birds. Behind the official, a waterfall cascaded like a silver wedding veil into a crystalline pool where goldfish dreamed. Sunlight splashed through wondrously shaped trees, palms and figs and species whose identity she'd never know. Everything about the moment was so foreign, so dreamy and drugging, that Kayla could easily imagine it a moment out of time.

Facing her, Matt stood by his father's side, hands clasped loosely one over the other. He was wearing a casual black cotton sports jacket, with a white shirt and gray trousers. The gray tie looked new. He was staring into middle space, his mind far away.

Kayla wondered where he was. He looked troubled, making it impossible for her not to think about her careless accusations yesterday that he still hadn't gotten over the failure of his marriage. He was a proud man, and of course he'd mind someone pointing out a short-coming, laying open a behavior pattern he thought he was concealing.

Unexpectedly Kayla noticed that Matt had focused on her with those troubled gray eyes. She smiled a small tentative smile, a reaching-out smile that begged him to stop being angry with her, to close the distance she'd stupidly created with yesterday's misplaced anger. And miracle of miracles, he smiled back. Every cell in her body suddenly seemed to pulse with heat.

His keen gray eyes swept over her. She thought she presented an attractive picture. Her dress was un-abashedly feminine, filmy voile with Venice lace in a shade of pale blue that complemented her fair coloring. She'd fussed with her makeup and tortured her hair, brushing it until it crackled and gleamed in loose golden waves.

She couldn't help wondering what Matt saw when he looked at her. Neither could she keep from acknowledging that anticipation of his reaction had utterly consumed her while she'd dressed.

Their eyes met again and held. Yes, she'd wanted him to find her attractive. He was the reason she'd fussed. More than that, she'd wanted him to *want* her, too. But why? It was such a senseless thing to want. They'd probably never see each other again after she went back to Chicago.

Between them Ruth was repeating the words, "For better or for worse, richer or poorer..." Some day soon, if she and Frank continued on their present course, Kayla would be reciting those same vows herself. Her balance grew a little weavy at the thought, and she clung to her visual connection with Matt to steady herself.

"In sickness and in health, till death do us part."

Matt had spoken those vows once himself, and undoubtedly meant every last syllable. Kayla watched the dance of leaf shadow on his rawboned cheek, saw coins of water light glitter in his thick dark hair, and thought, *The woman who left this man was stark raving mad.*

With a start Kayla heard the official speak the words, "I now pronounce you husband and wife." Good heavens, the ceremony was over. Philip was pressing a kiss to Ruth's cheek, and the semicircle of onlookers was applauding. She shook off her stupor and stepped forward to join in the congratulations.

"Congratulations, Dad." Matt gripped his father's hand in both of his, then turned to Ruth and hugged her warmly. Kayla did the same.

In the tangle of arms and murmured best wishes, Kayla happened to glance at Matt. They were family now. Whatever else happened in their lives, she and Matt were family, linked by these two loving people. For some reason, that thought cheered her immensely.

They spent another hour in the gardens, strolling the paths, admiring the lush plantings and taking pictures.

Ruth and Philip walked together arm in arm, leaving Kayla and Matt, by default, to fall into each other's company. Still feeling awkward after yesterday's fray, they didn't say anything of consequence.

The older couple paused by a wishing pool, its floor paved with coins. Giggling like teenagers, they leaned over the rail and tossed in two more. A safe ten feet away, Kayla and Matt only watched.

"Aren't you going to make a wish, too?" Ruth inquired.

Matt shrugged, while Kayla forced a chuckle and said, "We're too cheap to throw away our money."

"Oh, for heaven's sake." Ruth huffed, but she was too happy today to argue. She and Philip simply moved on, leaving Kayla and Matt to do as they pleased.

Feeling more awkward than ever, Kayla stepped to the rail and stared at the still-rippling water, wondering about this reluctance to partake of something as harmless as making a wish.

Matt rested his forearms on the rail beside her. "I used to make wishes when I was a kid. I loved to make wishes."

She nodded. "Twinkle, twinkle, and all that stuff."

"Hm. Somewhere along the way, though, I stopped— maybe when I realized stars and wishing pools didn't have much to do with dreams coming true."

"Oh, I don't know. I can remember standing at my window when I was in fifth grade and wishing I'd make the honor roll, and it happened."

Matt breathed out a laugh. "Because you wanted it to happen and probably worked your tail off to get there."

She smiled. "You're right. Once you plant the idea of success in your head..."

"Exactly. Positive thinking. Goal setting. That's all it is."

They gazed into the sun dazzle on the pool, and Kayla wondered, so why not now? Why not just pull a coin from her purse, make a wish and toss the dumb thing in? It was easy.

No, it wasn't, came the resounding reply from her heart. What would she wish for? Success for her stores? A beautiful wedding? A long, happy marriage? Bright, healthy children? Those were the logical choices at this point in her life.

Without realizing she was speaking, she softly murmured, "Be careful what you wish for."

Close beside her, Matt finished, "Because it might come true."

As if dragged by a gravitational pull, she turned to look at him. He did the same. And suddenly all the concerns he'd triggered during their talk on the patio came surging forth. "Oh, Matt, I *am* scared. You were right. And that's the reason I was such a witch yesterday."

A smile warmed his eyes. "I know."

"I don't know who I am anymore or where I'm going."

He lifted his hand, and the backs of his fingers drifted along her cheek. "Maybe you're not as confused as you think. Seems to me your participation in this wedding is a step in a very decided direction."

She shivered—from his meaning? Or was it his touch?

"The only uncertainty now is how far you're willing to go."

Implications hung in the air between them, implications he couldn't possibly mean—could he?

Lost in his eyes, Kayla felt caught in a spell, and in that instant she understood another reason—perhaps the real reason—she'd been so angry and unreasonable yesterday. No matter how adamantly she vowed to guard herself against Matt's appeal, her emotions apparently had a mind all their own. She had no defense against her vulnerability to him. Her head could lecture all it wanted, but her heart did just what it pleased.

Right now it was racing away. In excitement? she wondered. No, it was fear, fear of the powerful, mysterious bond that linked her with this man, the bond that was whispering louder and clearer as time went by that she was in love with him.

But why was he looking at her with such grave concern? And had his breathing stalled?

"Matthew?" Philip's voice seemed to come to them from a long distance. She blinked languidly.

Matt swallowed and reluctantly pulled his gaze from hers. "Yes?"

"Do us a favor and take our picture?"

They pulled in deep drafts of air and turned. "Be right there."

From the Garden of the Groves, Matt drove them to lunch at an isolated restaurant with a deck right on the beach. In their wedding finery they were clearly overdressed. They sat on hard wooden benches at a weatherworn table, while pesky seagulls stepped along the rail like gymnasts on a balance beam. But the food was excellent, the champagne cold and bubbly and the view beyond compare.

From there they went directly to the airport.

"We'll call when we return tomorrow night," Philip reminded them.

And Matt assured, "We'll be at the house waiting."

"Oh, and don't forget the buffet show at the hotel down the beach tonight. We left the tickets on the dining room table."

"You didn't have to do that, Dad."

"We know. But we thought you'd be a little lost for something to do without us around to liven things up."

"Well, thank you." Matt smiled. "It was very thoughtful of you."

"Now remember—" Ruth wagged her finger "—play nice."

"Get going." Kayla shooed them out the terminal door. Matt and Kayla waited until the plane took off, then slowly turned and began walking toward the exit.

"Well, looks like it's just you and me, kid," Matt drawled, smiling at her.

Kayla tried to ignore the sense of expectancy that bubbled inside her. Yes, they were now alone, and would be for more than twenty-four hours.

"So, what do you want to do?" he asked.

She pushed through the door. "First thing, I want to change into something more comfortable."

"Good idea. And second?"

She caught her lip between her teeth. "I want to call home and tell my father what just happened."

Matt stopped. "Are you sure?"

"Yes."

"But Ruth has volunteered to go back with you."

"I know, but at her age, with her recent health problems, she shouldn't have to go through anything so stressful. Telling my father she got married is my problem anyway, my responsibility. The least I can do is call, get the worst over with. That'll give him time to adjust to the news before we arrive."

For a fleeting moment, a small inner voice told her she was crazy. Her father was going to lambaste her. But Matt's eyes had lit with quiet admiration, and that was all she needed to know she'd made the right decision.

CHAPTER TEN

KAYLA watched her toes curl into the rug while she waited for the call to go through. Finally she heard a click, and then, "Good afternoon. Brayton Clockworks."

She stood at immediate attention, her pulse whooshing in her ears. Her father himself had answered the office phone.

"H-hi, Dad."

"Kayla?"

"Yes."

"Well, young lady, you finally remembered to call."

The whooshing grew to a roar. "Sorry 'bout that, Dad. Things've been kinda hectic here."

"Is that supposed to be an excuse?" The reprimand in her father's voice bit into her. Sweat trickled down her ribs.

"Well?" he demanded. "Are you going to tell me what's going on?"

She glanced toward the patio where Matt had politely retreated. He was sitting under a fig tree, holding a book, but he didn't seem to be reading. Was he watching her from behind his dark glasses? She hoped so. Crazy as it was, she felt he was lending her strength. She took a calming breath and said, "That's why I called, Dad."

Lloyd took the news worse than she'd expected.

"Your grandmother has done *what?*" he exploded.

Kayla tried to explain, tried to justify her reasons for supporting Ruth's decision to get married, tried to describe the old couple's contentment and joy, but her father wasn't buying any of it. Throughout her stum-

147

bling speech, he peppered the line with invective, finishing off with a bitter, "I should've sent Gordon."

Tears sprang to her eyes, but at least her voice remained even when she replied, "I'm sure Gordon would've reacted to the situation exactly as I did."

"Not likely, young lady. Not likely."

She blotted her eyes on her sleeve. "In any case, I'll be home day after tomorrow. Gran will be with me. I hope, for her sake, you'll be calm and more open-minded." And before he could add to the pain already overflowing her heart, she stammered a hasty goodbye and cradled the receiver.

She didn't move, just stood with her arms hanging limp at her sides, staring at the phone, while a crippling sense of failure overwhelmed her. Failure, incompetence and unlovability.

She didn't hear the door, only knew that Matt was with her almost instantly, pulling her against him, holding her close. Her throat ached, but she felt too numb even to move, let alone cry.

"It's all right," he whispered, holding her tighter.

She pressed into his warmth and security, her jaw clenched, eyes tightly closed.

"It's okay," Matt reassured softly, stroking her back. "You did it. It's over."

She rocked her forehead on his collarbone. "No, it isn't okay, and it is not over. He was very displeased with me, Matt, very upset."

"Give him time, Kayla. I'm sure once he's thought about it, he'll see the bright side."

She lifted her head and gave him a doubtful look. "What bright side?"

Under his half-closed lids his eyes began to glimmer. "I bet Lloyd has always wished he had a brother. I know I always did."

Kayla frowned in puzzlement, and then almost choked on a laugh. "Good God, you and my father are stepbrothers now."

Matt smiled, but the warmth in his eyes didn't seem to have much to do with his discovery of a new brother. "Which has to make you and me something to each other, though I'll be damned if I can figure out what." He framed her face with his large gentle hands and brushed her cheeks with his thumbs.

Her eyes searched his, long and deep. Yes, they were something to each other, all right, but what?

Their mood changed, subtly at first, away from sympathetic companionship, and then swiftly to heartpounding awareness. Awareness of how close they were standing, of their mingled scents, of the heat building between them.

Her gaze roamed his features—the particular way he combed his hair off his brow, the grain of his skin, the small intriguing indentation that shaped the bow of his upper lip. He was so incredibly—what? Handsome? Of course he was handsome, but that wasn't the reason she couldn't get enough of looking at him. Surely she'd met handsome men before, perhaps even more handsome, but she hadn't felt this peculiar addiction. This went deeper than a mere reaction to pleasantly arranged features. She seriously thought she could go on looking at him forever and never lose her fascination.

For the second time that day, Kayla was assailed by the fear that she'd fallen in love with this man, but the fear had deepened. For heaven only knew what reason, Matt was physically attracted to her, too. She'd known it two nights ago while sitting on the patio, and she knew it now. The question that remained, however, was would he decide to act on that attraction, and what would she do if he did?

She watched him swallow and then, blinking, look aside. He dropped his hands from her face and eased away from her. "Feeling better?" he asked.

She pressed her lips together, both relieved that he'd had the good sense to end the moment and annoyed that she hadn't done so herself. "Yes, I do. Thanks, Matt."

He shrugged dismissively. "So, what now? What would you like to do with the rest of this day?"

Kayla caught her lip between her teeth, thinking. They should keep active. Their time alone together would pass faster if they did. Suddenly she snapped her fingers. "I have an idea."

"Are you sure you want to do this?" Matt muttered as they sat on the seawall up the beach in front of one of the large hotels, filling out the form that released the parasailing company from liability should they get hurt.

"Chicken," Kayla taunted, even though she was having lots of second thoughts herself.

After they'd filled out the form and paid their fee, they splashed through the water and slipped into a motor boat, joining a wiry Bahamian youth sitting at the wheel. A moment later, they were speeding away from shore to a launching raft where a small crew awaited them.

Four other boats were zooming around the raft in what appeared a dangerously close pattern, their parasailers flying like human kites begging to be tangled.

"Who's going first?" one of the crew asked. Kayla's stomach lurched.

"I will," Matt offered. She let out a sigh of relief.

The boy helped Matt into a special harness while another spread open a colorful nylon parachute. The boat driver, meanwhile, had positioned his craft at a short distance. A cable trailed loosely from the stern to Matt's harness.

"Are you ready?" the attendant called.

Matt gave a thumbs-up, even while the boat engine revved and the cable tautened. As instructed he took two running steps. On the second, his foot didn't even touch the raft. The parasail had billowed, and he was aloft.

Kayla watched him go, her heart in her throat. He rose much faster than she had expected and before long was so high she could barely discern him from the other parasailers.

Much too soon for her liking, however, his time in the air was over. With a practiced maneuver, the boat driver brought the cable to the raft, and then Matt was being reeled in. Soon he was safely landed and disengaged.

"Well?" Kayla asked, while the young Bahamians scurried around her, hooking the still-billowing parachute to her harness.

"Out of this world," Matt replied, grinning.

"Really? It isn't scary?"

Before he could answer, one of the youths said a musical, "Bye-bye" and waved at her. She inhaled a screech, feeling the tug forward.

By the time Matt's laughter reached her, she was twenty feet off the water and rising. "Of course it's scary," he called. "That's what makes it so much fun."

She looked at the boat speeding ahead of her, letting out more line. She snapped shut her eyes and tightened her grip on the cables near her ears.

After a few seconds, though, she realized the folly in what she was doing, namely, wasting precious moments of her ride. She opened her eyes, deciding instead to soak up every sensation she could.

Actually the takeoff had been much smoother than she'd expected, and this rising into the air wasn't really so bad. In fact, it was kind of nice. Gentle. Like floating to the top of a Ferris wheel.

She began to relax, and as she did she became aware of her broadening perspective. She could see miles of white beach, sunbathers mere specks of color against the sand. She could see inland over hotels, houses, roadways and trees. But what fascinated her most was the water below, the vivid turquoise and aqua and bottle-green of the water. It was so clear she could see right to the bottom, to gardens of seaweed, coral, even the occasional large fish.

Awed by the view, she wished she'd brought a camera. It would be nice for her father to see this. He never went anywhere, not even on business; he always sent Gordon.

Abruptly her heart grew heavy under the memory of her father's hurtful words on the phone. Why did he always have to find fault with her? *Did* she continually make mistakes? *Was* she stupid? Was she homely or unlovable? Or did he, as she'd always suspected, secretly resent her for causing her mother's death? She pressed her lips tight, fighting against her rising tears.

The wind rushed at her face, whipping her hair and reminding her where she was. No, she wouldn't let her father's resentment ruin this experience. Matt was right; this was her life, the only one she was going to get, and the only person she had to please was herself.

She looked down at the boat and guessed she was now at around three hundred feet. Instead of frightened, she felt proud of herself for doing something that defied logic and gravity and all common sense.

Ever so slowly she loosened her death grip on the cables and, by inches, spread her arms. When they were halfway extended, she laughed nervously. So far nothing had happened; she was still securely strapped, still safely seated in her harness. She continued to unfold, and when her arms were fully stretched, she grinned from ear to ear. She felt like a bird, a great colorful seabird, embracing the wind.

How long she glided in that fashion she wasn't sure, but much too soon she felt herself descending, the line being reeled in.

"Well?" Matt smiled as her feet touched down.

She whooped in answer. Words simply weren't adequate for what she felt.

He laughed. "Hold onto the feeling, Kayla."

They exchanged a meaningful glance, and she said, "I'll try."

They spent the remainder of that afternoon lazing on the beach. Kayla had her left ankle fitted with a coral bracelet and finally gave in to the offer of, "Braids, lady?" She got several, in fact, with flashy gold beads, and then challenged Matt to do the same.

"My hair's too short," he protested.

But the woman who'd done Kayla's assured him it was not. She could even braid chest hair, she claimed, and had done so often. Beards, too.

Matt gave her an arch look. "The head will do." He ended up with three tiny braids entwined with black beads.

Returning to the house, they found the dinner show tickets Philip had alluded to paper-clipped to a flyer that described the event. As Matt brushed his teeth, Kayla lounged in the bathroom doorway, reading.

"All you can eat. Traditional Bahamian entrees. A buffet delight. Followed by a live native review." She glanced up from her reading. "What d'ya think?"

Chewing around his brush, he answered, "Better than a dead native review."

She swatted him with the flyer.

"What time?" he asked.

"Dinner, six-thirty. Show's at eight."

After glancing at his watch, he nodded. "I'll be ready. Just have to shave. What about you?"

"No problem, mon. Just have to change."

"For the better, I hope."

She groaned before turning and heading for her room.

Matt was already outside when she came downstairs. He was sitting on the patio, legs stretched, hands linked atop his head.

"What do you think of the outfit?" she asked, turning for his assessment. Along with a host of other concessions she'd made during the past week, she'd bought a loosely flowing, calf-length dress of natural cotton gauze. The gathered skirt flared and floated as she turned, the golden beads in her long golden hair clicking a soft seduction.

Matt sat up and smiled appreciatively. "Nice. Very, very nice." He pulled out a chair for her. "Sit down a minute, Kayla. I have something to ask you."

Her curiosity stirred, along with a healthy dose of apprehension. "What's the matter?"

"I have a favor to ask."

"Fire away."

"Be warned, it's going to seem an odd request."

"What, for heaven's sake? You look so solemn, you're scaring me."

His gaze became even more intense. "Not half as much as you're scaring me, sweetheart."

Her pulse hammered. "So, wh-what—" She couldn't speak.

He reached across the table and ran two fingertips over her knuckles. "Will you take off your ring tonight?"

She blinked repeatedly as if that might clarify her hearing.

"The sapphire Frank gave you. Will you do me the favor of not wearing it?" He looked right into her eyes, compelling her to look back and know that this was important. "Just for tonight. You can put it back on tomorrow."

"But why? I don't understand."

"It's occurred to me that I'm probably going to say some things to you tonight, and maybe do things, that would be better said and done if you weren't encumbered by such an obvious reminder of him."

Every inch of her seemed to throb with delicious panic. Several seconds passed before she could say, "But taking off a ring won't change anything."

He grinned. "You wouldn't want to bet on that, would you?"

"Matthew Reed, this is the craziest—"

His grin disappeared. "Kayla, we've been striking sparks off each other all week. Until now, we've tried to pretend they didn't exist, but I don't want to do that anymore." His eyes burned with a fervor that both frightened and thrilled her. "I think we owe it to ourselves to explore those sparks, see where they take us."

"But that's the problem. They can't take us anywhere."

He smiled softly. "Only to heaven and back."

She shivered, hot and weak under the seduction of his words. "But for how long? Everything is so complicated."

"Damn the complications. I'll worry about them later." He gripped her hand, squeezed her fingers. "We don't have much time, sweetheart. If not now, when?"

When, indeed? This was their only night alone, and they'd be leaving here in another day. Reeling under his seductive words and intimate gaze, Kayla emitted a shaky sigh. "All right. It's crazy but, all right, if it'll make you happy." She removed her ring, then looked at him uncertainly. He glanced toward the house.

Shrugging, she went inside and left the ring on the coffee table. *What did I just agree to?* she wondered. But already a blissful headiness was streaming through her, an intimation that the most wonderful thing in her life was about to unfold.

Matt said nothing more regarding their strangely frank conversation, but his mood had changed. He no longer tried to conceal or control his reactions to her. When he spoke, he looked directly into her eyes. When he smiled, the world shrank to a bubble that contained only them.

They walked to the hotel along the shoreline, shoes hooked carelessly from their fingers, a ripe sun setting at their back. A few hair braiders and jewelry vendors lounged on the beach walls, talking and laughing among themselves in the quiet lee of their business day. Sandpipers stamped their prints on the wet sand.

Hand in hand, Matt and Kayla kept their pace slow, as desultory as the day's lingering heat. There was no reason to hurry, because with Matt she felt she'd already reached her destination.

They climbed the steps to the hotel grounds and were drawn to a pavilion by the sound of a steel band quietly playing "Land of the Sea and Sun". Dozens of tables were set for dinner, with pink table linens and fresh flower centerpieces. Unfortunately, there were no tables for two, and they had no choice but to sit with another couple.

Nevertheless, even through dinner conversation, Matt somehow continued to make her feel they existed in a world apart. She wasn't sure how he did it, how he managed to talk with the middle-aged couple from Ottawa and still wrap her in a sense of undivided attention. Was it his deep, lingering stare? His habit of leaning in when he talked? Whatever it was, Kayla began to feel light-headed and didn't want it to stop.

As advertised, the meal was a buffet delight. Matt and Kayla both went back for seconds, although, to be honest, she was hardly aware of eating. The review passed with an equally dreamlike quality. Singers, fire eaters, limbo dancers, steel drum players, all flowed before her in a happy haze.

The finale to the show was something neither Kayla nor Matt had expected, however, and it caught their full attention. It was a Junkanoo parade.

Junkanoo, the master of ceremonies explained, was a native festivity similar to Mardi Gras, celebrated on Boxing Day and then again at New Year's. "It starts before dawn when the sound of drums, horns and whistles begins to lift from the far hills."

Even as he said this, the sound he described rose from behind the stage. A surprised murmur rolled through the audience.

"And as the sound comes closer," the emcee continued, "you begin to see the men in their costumes, and then you know it's Junkanoo!"

Kayla gaped in surprised delight as a parade of about thirty men moved into view. The sound they made was deafening, deafening and hypnotic—wildly beaten drums, shrilling whistles, blaring horns. The men wore fanciful headdresses and brightly painted paper skirts, and danced frenetically as they made their way past the stage into the audience.

"Everybody up," the emcee urged. "Time to jump in the line."

Kayla looked at Matt. He shrugged, took her hand and got to his feet.

The Junkanoo line snaked between the tables, and Matt and Kayla, together with the rest of the dinner patrons, went with it. Caught in the primitive beat, it was impossible not to throw reserve to the wind, impossible not to release one's inhibitions and act just a little silly.

Hip to hip, arms loosely draped across each other's backs, Matt and Kayla moved forward, dancing to the rhythm of the drums.

"Matt, I think we're doing the merengue again!" she said, as the parade wended its way right into the hotel proper.

"That damn beat permeates everything here." He laughed.

The parade went through several lobbies and lounges, rocking the building and astounding guests with its racket. But when they reached the main lobby, the musicians stopped, bowed and made their exit through the front door.

"What a clever way to say the party's over." Kayla laughed. "They get us out of our seats, away from the pavilion and abandon us in a lobby."

With his face still alight with almost boyish pleasure, Matt put his arm across her shoulder and ushered her back the way they'd come. Outside, waiters were clearing tables, musicians packing instruments. But the party didn't feel over. Making their way around the pavilion and through the pool area, they fell again into their personalized merengue step, which dissolved in a fit of laughter.

When they reached the stairs leading down to the beach, they paused, struck by the view.

"A full moon," Matt murmured. "How perfect."

"Mm." Kayla breathed deeply. The fragrance of bougainvillea sweetened the warm night air, blending with the salty tang of the sea. She felt besotted with the beauty of this place. Its rhythms and scents and tastes seemed indelibly branded into her sense memory.

At least, she hoped they were. She never wanted to forget the week she'd just spent.

Some of the lights on the path behind them were directed toward the beach, illuminating the water and sand. Kayla noticed that, standing where they were, she and Matt cast a long fused shadow that reached across the sand and rippled over the curling waves.

"If we absolutely must return to the States," she said wistfully, almost to herself, "then let's at least leave our shadows here."

Matt's arm tightened around her. "A deal."

They meandered up the beach, talking quietly, occasionally singing snatches of songs that had been performed that night. At other times they said nothing. It wasn't an easy silence. A sense of charged excitement fizzed through Kayla's blood, anticipation as strong as a child's on Christmas morning.

Being in Matt's company—that's what was doing it. Just being with him made her too incredibly light-headed and happy.

Nearing the house, their steps slowed and soon came to a stop altogether. Matt turned her in his arms, folding her close.

"Matt, I'm not sure this is wise," she murmured. But it was token resistance. There was nothing Kayla wanted more than to be in Matt's embrace.

"Lady, I *know* this isn't wise, but I can't help myself. You've got me bewitched." He smoothed her hair, his eyes burning over her with longing. With his hands still cupped around her head, he lowered his lips to hers.

When he finally eased away, a hard pulse was beating visibly at the base of his throat. "Oh, lady, you do pack a punch."

Small streamers of satisfaction tickled her ego. She smiled. "Want to try for a knockout?"

Desire flared in his eyes and he pulled her tighter. "Don't say such things. A guy could get the wrong..." But he didn't finish. He didn't seem able. He simply surrendered to need.

This kiss was more powerful than the first, and seemed to go on forever. Matt's fingers tangled in her hair. Hers tangled in his. He explored the curves of her back. She did the same, their bodies lifting and straining with mounting urgency all the while.

This had to be the closest thing to heaven, Kayla thought, as Matt angled his mouth to take deeper possession of her. And the next moment she was thinking, No, *this* is the closest thing to heaven.

By the time they pulled apart, she was a lost woman. Lost in the heat pulsing through her, lost in the magic that was Matt Reed. She clung to him, trembling and weak and wondering why this wondrous reaction had never struck her before. She felt more alive, more sensuous and beautiful, than she'd ever felt in her life.

"Kayla, Kayla," he whispered hoarsely, tucking her close. "You're driving me out of mind. Have I told you that lately?"

She smiled, soaring with happiness. This was better than she'd expected—far, far better. Surely the things he was saying indicated he felt more for her than a simple physical attraction.

"What's happened to us this week?" he asked. "This was the last thing I expected to have happen."

"Meaning what?" She looked at him coquettishly. "That I'm such a dog you couldn't possibly imagine being attracted to me?"

He laughed, hugging her closer, rocking her. She loved the deep rumble of his chest, the woodsy scent of his aftershave. "You still don't have any idea how beautiful you are, do you?" His hands pressed along her spine, his gaze caressing her, hot and searching.

"I love being flattered, but really..."

He shook his head fractionally. "You have a quiet beauty, Kayla. Some guys might miss it, blind guys, stupid guys. I pride myself on being neither. Your beauty is the kind that whispers, and then it haunts, resonating deep inside when a guy least expects it. And make no mistake, you do haunt me."

She *haunted* him? Kayla shivered under the tender assault of his words. "And you haunt me, Matt," she whispered, finally giving over what she'd wanted to say since she was a girl. "You have forever."

He pulled her to him in a move that was almost rough in its sudden unleashed fervor and covered her mouth with his, tasting of her, making her cry softly with the sudden desire that rocketed through her.

He pressed his hands along her back, down and down, until they were at her hips and he was gripping tight, trembling fistfuls of gauzy skirt. "If we don't do something else," he said raggedly, "this dress isn't going to stay on your back too much longer."

Kayla suspected she should be alarmed, but instead she grinned like the Cheshire cat. "Is that a promise?"

His eyes narrowed and glinted devilishly. "Ooh, you little tease."

When he moved to grab her, she pushed him away with a firm shove to the chest. He stumbled backward while she laughed and made a run for the house. She hadn't taken two steps, however, before he caught her wrist and pulled her back, swinging her wide so that she sailed over the sand in great loping strides, stumbling, tripping and finally losing her balance altogether. He toppled with her, a tangle of arms and legs and laughter rolling on the packed wet sand at the waterline.

"You savage!" Pinned to the sand, she laughed, gazing into Matt's closely looming face. "Why didn't my grandmother tell me you were into assault and battery on helpless women?"

Moonlight silvered his muscular shoulders and thick dark hair, the black beads falling over his temple lending a primitive touch. "Lady, if there's anything you're not, it's helpless."

A wave splashed over her feet, into her shoes and up to her thighs. "Ugh. My dress is getting soaked." She heaved with all her might, tossing him onto his back, knowing full well that if he hadn't wanted to go, he wouldn't have. Another wave slid shoreward, and she felt Matt flinch under her.

"Aha! How do *you* like getting wet and man-handled?" Her words came in short, laughing gasps as she draped her torso and one leg over him to nail him down. Moonlight made crystals of his gray eyes.

"Getting wet I can do without, but this manhandling thing—" he laughed and she bounced with the rise and fall of his chest "—now that part's beginning to turn me on."

"Everything turns you on, Matthew."

"True," he said, rolling her over so abruptly her breath whooshed out of her when her back hit the sand. "Especially sassy little blondes with gold beads in their hair and lips that were made for ravishing."

By the time he'd finished saying this, Kayla was no longer smiling. And neither was Matt. They both lay still, exploring each other with their eyes, and then slowly Matt lowered his head and kissed her. Another wave rolled in, but Kayla was barely aware of it. She wound her arms around Matt's shoulders and completely forgot the outside world. Only one thing consumed her—this man whom she loved. He'd become the center of her universe this week, and the thought of never seeing him again was already tearing her in two.

She clung to him, returning his kiss with a fire born of desperation. No, what they had between them couldn't end with this night. It wouldn't. It was too strong, too deep. This was just the beginning. They'd find a way to continue seeing each other. They would. Anything was possible once you set your mind to it. And tonight everything felt possible.

Matt got to his feet, pulling her with him. Her dress hung sodden and sandy, molding itself to her curves. With a shudder of control, he tucked her under his arm and started up the beach toward the house.

Her heart hammered. Were they about to do what she thought they were about to do? Were they ready? Was *she* ready?

As Matt closed the patio doors behind them, muting the night sounds of crickets and surf, Kayla became aware that the buzzer was ringing, signaling that someone was at the front gate. She looked at Matt, he looked at her, and they frowned.

"Oh, no." Alarm raced through her. "You don't suppose something's happened to my grandmother?"

They hurried to the door, brushing sand out of their hair and slapping their clothing. "We look a mess," Matt cautioned.

"I don't care." Kayla ran ahead of him up the drive. She was almost at the gate when suddenly she stopped. Everything stopped. Her footsteps, her breathing, her heart. For there on the other side of the gate, his eyes ablaze and his bearing icy, stood her father.

CHAPTER ELEVEN

KAYLA stared through the bars of the gate, immobilized. Her father stared back.

"Kayla, is that you?" He looked positively owlish with shock. She realized then that the lamps atop the gateposts were casting more than sufficient light for him to see the beaded tangles in her hair, the sand weighing down her wet, clinging dress.

"Good God, girl! What's happened to you? What's been going on here? Let me in."

Humiliation sickened her.

Matt stepped forward, wearing a scowl even blacker than Lloyd's. "What are you doing here, Mr. Brayton?"

"I'm speaking to my daughter, do you mind?"

"Yes, as a matter of fact, I do."

Kayla shook herself out of her daze. "It's all right, Matt." She laid a hand on his arm. "Dad, what *are* you doing here?"

Lloyd's reproachful gaze moved over her. "I've come to get your grandmother."

She realized that wasn't what she really wanted to know. "How did you find this place?"

"I phoned Frank. He told me."

"Frank?" Matt swung on her. "And how the devil did *he* find out?"

Kayla winced, remembering her phone call to him the night she'd arrived. Matt swore under his breath, while Lloyd rattled the gate.

"Are you ever going to let me in?"

Kayla's head was beginning to hurt. "Gran isn't here."

164

"Isn't here? What have you done now, Reed?"

"Calm down, Dad. Gran and Philip have simply gone on an overnight trip. They'll be back tomorrow."

"You mean the two of you are here alone?"

Kayla tried to neaten her appearance by tucking her hair behind her ears. "Yes." Her voice was pitifully thin.

Matt gripped a bar in one fist and leaned, nose to nose with the man outside the gate. "Mr. Brayton, it's late. Kayla and I have had a long day, and we'd like to shower and get some sleep now. I suggest you go find a nice hotel room and do the same."

Lloyd's eyes narrowed to slits. "Ooh, you're begging for it, Reed. How about I come back with the police?"

"How about you take a hike?"

"Stop it," Kayla shouted. "Just stop." She ran her palms down her wet, gritty skirt. "Matt, let him in."

His angry breath fanned her face. "Are you crazy?"

"Matt! That's my father. It's late and he must be tired. We can't leave him out on the street."

Matt muttered a few more oaths but finally did as she asked.

"Thank you," Lloyd said, his voice arrogant with sarcasm.

Matt hit him with a look so quelling that even in his considerable anger Lloyd couldn't hold it.

Coming into the house, into even brighter light, Kayla braced herself for more argument. She knew her and Matt's appearance was going to take some explaining. But Lloyd only looked at her and shook his head. The disappointment in his eyes almost broke her heart.

"Have a seat," Matt directed brusquely. "We'll be down in a few minutes." Then taking Kayla's arm, he tugged gently.

"What?" She looked up, uncomprehending.

"Let's go clean up."

"Oh. Yes. Right." Still feeling her father's reproof, she climbed the stairs.

"You can use our shower," Matt said. "I'll use the one in the master bath."

She entered the bathroom, dreading to face the mirror. With good reason, she realized, when she took in the puffiness of her lips and the red blotches where Matt's beard had abraded her skin.

She cried in the shower, the reasons a blur. She was humiliated, of course. She felt like a teenager who'd been caught making out in the backseat of a car.

But she was also disappointed that her time with Matt had been cut short. She knew she ought to be ashamed of that particular attitude, and she supposed she was, but she was also deeply, painfully disappointed.

And angry. Oh, yes, anger was there, as well. Her father had no right to do this to her, to come here with his lack of faith in her, undercutting her confidence, making her feel she couldn't do anything right.

And he definitely had no right to upset her grand-mother. Newly married, relaxed and enjoying herself for the first time in years, Ruth shouldn't have to be subjected to the tumult her son was sure to cause.

This last thought straightened Kayla's spine and sparked a sudden protectiveness toward Ruth. By the time Matt tapped at her door, her anger had thoroughly galvanized.

"Are you ready to go down?" He was wearing jeans, a white shirt and a battle-ready scowl.

"Yes. Yes, I am." She tightened the sash of her bathrobe. "But I've been thinking, maybe you'd better just go to bed."

"Uh-uh. No way."

"Please, Matt. I can handle my father, but not with you there, too. If you go down, we'll probably end up fighting at cross-purposes, and, quite frankly, I'm in no mood for that tonight."

He studied her flashing eyes, her tensed mouth, her eyes again. "Are you sure you'll be okay?"

She nodded stolidly. "After he and I talk, I'll settle him in Ruth and Phil's room. Is that okay with you?"

Matt looked reluctant but finally nodded. "Don't take any guff."

"I won't. See you in the morning." She was walking away when he caught her by the wrist and pulled her back. She steadied herself with a hand to his warm chest. His gaze captured hers and grew smoldering.

For a second she thought he was going to kiss her, but then he just smiled in regret and murmured, "It would've been out of this world. You know that, don't you?"

Pleasurably shaken, and curiously heartened, she went downstairs.

It was a long night, and one of the strangest Kayla had ever lived through. It began with Kayla telling Lloyd about Ruth's wedding, followed immediately by Lloyd sailing into Kayla for allowing the marriage to happen. But her anger and determination to prevail soon had the situation turned around.

Kayla told her father how furious she was that he'd lied to her about Ruth's health, how puzzled she was to get here and find Ruth no more senile than she was—a little forgetful sometimes, but generally as sharp as ever. She also told him she knew about what he'd been doing—managing Ruth's household, restricting her activity, talking about a nursing home—and that she thought his behavior was appalling.

Of course, Lloyd didn't see things that way at all. He said he was only acting out of concern for his mother's health, and from the passion of his arguments, Kayla realized he believed he was telling the truth. He continued to defend his actions, in fact, until Kayla told him the news of Ruth's plan to relinquish her position at Brayton's to him when she returned to Boston. That settled him down, amazingly so, and once he'd settled she had the opportunity to explain Ruth's side.

Kayla explained how his coddling behavior had made Ruth feel old and useless, and how Philip had just the opposite effect on her. Lloyd looked stunned, especially when Kayla told him that all Ruth had ever wanted from him was his trust that she was a worthwhile person who could still think for herself.

Kayla even got him to listen to a defense of Matt and Philip, although she suspected the credit went not so much to her powers of persuasion as to his realizing that Brayton's was going to stay in the family.

Rather than disparaging that fact, she used it to her advantage. She said Ruth would probably be furious if she found him here when she returned from her trip. She might even change her mind about signing over Brayton's. Paling, her father agreed to fly back to Boston on the first flight he could book the next day. He also agreed to welcome Ruth with a calm and accepting attitude.

Kayla sank into the sofa cushions with a sense of relief. It was nearly three in the morning, but she'd reached her objective, to keep Ruth from being upset and hurt.

But when she looked across the room at her father, she saw that he had been upset and hurt in the process.

"How did things get so out of hand, Kayla?" he asked, looking haggard with anguish. "How did *I* get so out of hand?"

Her heart went out to him. "I'm not sure, Dad, but if I were to guess, I'd say you let Brayton's take over your life."

Lloyd became defensive again. "Is that so wrong?"

"Well..." She took a deep breath and searched for a diplomatic way to say what she thought.

The next time Kayla glanced at the clock, it was four-fifteen. She was exhausted, but she wouldn't have traded this night for anything.

With as much tact as she could marshal, she had drawn her father into a reluctant conversation about himself. It became important to her that he see his recent behavior as skewed, his fear of losing Brayton's almost paranoid. He didn't agree with her perception until she pointed out how sanguine he'd become once he'd learned Brayton's would be signed over. Mortification then filled his expression.

Inevitably talk had led to his wife. He'd been a mere twenty-five at the time of her death. Such a young man, Kayla said. Why didn't he ever remarry? And he replied something vague about no woman ever being able to replace her mother.

They went round that particular issue for a while, during which time Kayla slipped in the suggestion that he'd purposely cluttered his life with work to heal the pain, or maybe to escape it, and without realizing it had drifted into a way of living that involved nothing but work. The parallel with Matt didn't escape her.

"You're still young, Dad," she said. "Maybe you ought to consider socializing more, taking up golf or tennis, maybe even going on an occasional vacation."

"Oh, no, I couldn't."

"Why not? Look at Gran. She's gained a whole new lease on life."

Laughing, Lloyd had finally agreed to give it some thought.

Now he pushed to his feet and yawned. "I think we ought to try and get a couple of hours' sleep."

"I think you're right, Dad." Kayla couldn't help giving him a hug. "I'm glad we had this talk."

For the first time in years he returned the hug with straightforward, unembarrassed affection. "I am, too." They began to walk toward the stairs. "I have one question, though." He paused, his smile waning. "What on earth were you and Matt Reed doing when I showed up?"

Memories, sluggish with tiredness, came creeping back—the dinner show, walking on the beach and kisses so wonderful that even now, just thinking about them, fire kindled in her veins. "We were, um, in a silly mood. We'd just come back from a dinner show at one of the big hotels and we decided to go for a swim, clothes and all."

A frown creased his brow. "Are you sure nothing else happened?"

"Nothing else happened," she replied, not able to meet his gaze. She wasn't sure why she didn't tell him the truth, except that he had enough adjustments to make for a while.

"Well, I hope not," he said. "You've got a wonderful man in Frank Schaeffer, a wonderful future awaiting you. I'd hate to see you mess it up by getting involved with a guy who's strictly a dead end."

She frowned. "What do you mean, a dead end?" Somehow she didn't think he was referring just to the fact that a thousand miles lay between her and Matt. Was he implying that she wasn't capable of interesting someone so dynamic?

Lloyd's answer was not what she expected. "Well, it's no secret he's in the process of reconciling with his wife."

Kayla went as still as the night. "What did you say?"

"Reconciling. With his wife. Hasn't he mentioned it?"

She could only shake her head.

"Typical of him." Lloyd scowled. "Fortunately, his ex isn't quite so tight-lipped about what goes on in her private life. The last time your brother went over to

Holland Advertising to see about an ad campaign for Brayton's, he ran into her."

"She still lives in the city?" Her stomach dropped.

"Oh, sure. And she mentioned to Gordon that she and Matt had been getting together to discuss the possibility of reuniting."

Every fiber of strength had left Kayla's body. Even her voice was weak and shaky when she said, "Are you sure?"

"Yes. Gordon saw them a few days later, having dinner at some restaurant on the waterfront. Kayla, are you all right?"

She roused herself out of her shock and smiled bravely. "Yes, I'm fine. I'm just a little surprised that Matt's never said anything. We've become ... good friends."

"Well, he must have his reasons." Lloyd stifled a yawn. "I really have to turn in, Kayla."

"Yes, of course. Good-night, Dad. I'll be up in a minute myself."

She waited until she heard the door at the top of the stairs shut before she turned and went outside. Leaning against the patio door, she took in deep gulps of warm night air to help stave off the despair creeping through her.

What a fool she'd been. What a blind fool. She should have known. The first time she and Matt had talked about his marriage, way back at Logan Airport, she'd seen so much suppressed emotion behind his set expression, she should have known. His marriage wasn't over. It was very much on his mind.

Without wanting to, Kayla took another mental leap, one that left her feverish and reaching for a chair for support. Why hadn't it occurred to her sooner? Matt still loved his wife. *That* was why he worked so dedicatedly, why he never got seriously involved with another woman. It wasn't just because he was afraid of being hurt again. He'd never stopped loving his wife.

And now they were getting back together.

Kayla dropped into a chaise, the same one she'd shared with Matt a few nights earlier. Everything made sense now, his pensive moods, the trouble in his eyes, especially during Ruth's wedding vows. He'd been thinking of his wife, of the vows they'd shared—and all the while she, Kayla, had been smiling at him, reaching out to him with her love, acting like a fool.

Oh, sure, he'd been attracted to her, she was still fairly certain of that. But apparently it was a shallow physical attraction, nothing more. For a while tonight her imagination had run off and led her to believe he felt more. But, really, had he ever done or said anything to corroborate her assumptions? Had he talked about the future or said he loved her?

Tonight he'd remarked that they needed to explore what existed between them. *If not tonight, when?* he'd said. But now his meaning came clear. This night was all they had, all he would allow them to have. In other words, there would be no more.

She was lucky her father had shown up when he had. If she and Matt had made love, she didn't think she'd ever heal from the pain of learning the truth. As it was, she'd still be hurt, but at least she could salvage her pride.

She could also help Matt. Putting a broken marriage back together couldn't be easy, and if she'd sidetracked him or caused him to doubt what he and his wife were doing, she was sorry. She'd remove herself, remove her moony stares and obvious adoration, and never bother him again. It would hurt, but it was what was best for Matt.

She closed her eyes, sighing. How close she'd come to telling him she was considering breaking up with

Frank, giving up her stores and returning to Boston. How close she'd come to thinking they had a future.

But she'd remedy that. She would. First thing tomorrow.

When Matt came downstairs, Kayla was still lying in the chaise, half-dozing. He sat in the chair beside her. She blinked open her eyes, squinting at the cloudless blue sky, then at him. Immediately pain contracted her heart.

"Have you been up all night?" he asked.

She stretched in false nonchalance. "Sort of."

Matt looked concerned. "How did it go?"

She was quiet a long while, not knowing where to begin. "Don't be surprised if you get an apology from my father today."

Matt's left eyebrow curled.

"He's also agreed to fly back to Boston before Ruth and Philip return."

"How'd you manage that? What did you say?"

"I think it was how I said it. I was angry, Matt. I don't think he's ever seen me angry before." Her bathrobe had come apart enough to partially reveal the T-shirt beneath. Matt reached over and with two fingers lifted the satiny material another inch. A smile curled one corner of his mouth as he read the slogan, Flying Free in Freeport.

She'd forgotten what she'd slipped on last night after her shower. The irony didn't escape her. Matt had urged her to take control of her life and cut free of the influence of her father, when all the while *he* was the one unable to follow his own advice. He was still tied to the past, and it seemed he always would be.

"So, it went well?"

"Yes. We had a really good talk. I got a lot off my chest."

Matt smiled an endearing, lopsided smile. "Kayla Brayton, you never cease to amaze me."

Kayla looked aside, frowning.

"What time is his flight?" Matt asked.

"We're going to call the airport and arrange that this morning."

"And we're not going to tell Ruth he was here?"

"Not a word. What I thought you might tell her is, I called him and turned his attitude around during a long phone conversation."

Matt's expression clouded. "What you thought *I* could tell her?"

"Yes." Kayla chewed on her thumbnail, not looking at him.

"Why can't you tell her yourself?"

The heaviness in her heart deepened. "Matt, let's go down to the beach."

Watching her guardedly, he rose and walked with her to the gate. They didn't say anything until they were at the water's edge, and by then Matt's expression had become as dark as hers.

"I'm thinking of returning to Chicago directly from here, today," she said, gazing out over the sun-shot water.

She heard Matt pull in a long breath, a breath that he didn't release.

"But only if you agree to tell Ruth that I had to leave," she said quickly. "That an emergency arose."

"And is she supposed to return to Boston alone?"

She cast a stealthy glance his way. His face had hardened into an unreadable mask.

"I was thinking, you have to go back anyway..."

"I see."

"I'm really not needed there. My father won't give her any trouble, he promised."

"So, you're leaving. Going back to Frank and your stores and your ten-year plans."

"Yes." A sense of finality hung in the air. "Vacation's over. Time to get back to real life." Although her heart was breaking, for his sake she tried to keep her tone light.

From the corner of her eye she saw Matt cross his arms, shift his weight, tap his fingers. "Answer one thing, Kayla. What about what happened between us this week?"

She'd hoped he wouldn't bring that up. She didn't even understand why he did, unless he felt obliged to play out his part right to the end, to lessen her sense of having been used.

"It's been wonderful, Matt. I want you to know that. I had the time of my life, but this week has been an unnatural situation. We've been living in a vacation setting, a romantic tropical paradise. We let ourselves get carried away." She shrugged as if getting carried away held the same level of importance as getting a suntan. "But your life is back in Boston and mine's in Chicago. It's time to return. We always knew this day would come. Didn't we?"

She waited and waited, and finally he said, "Yes."

His admission was almost her undoing. What had she expected him to say? No? Even if his wife didn't exist, even if Kayla gave up her stores and returned to Boston, was there any guarantee she and Matt would pick up where they left off here? Would she still appeal to him without the backdrop of palm trees and lavender skies? Would she be as happy and carefree when the steel drums faded and the roar of traffic took their place? Would he?

Just then her father called to her from the gate. She turned gratefully and waved. "Be right there, Dad."

Matt was still staring out over the water, eyes fixed and narrowed, jaw clenched. "Do you want me to give you a ride to the airport?"

"Would you?" Apparently he wasn't going to argue against her leaving. But then, why would he?

"Of course. And don't worry about Ruth. I'll take care of everything."

Kayla's throat was closing painfully. If she didn't walk off soon, she was going to make a colossal fool of herself. "Well, you keep practicing that merengue," she said, backing away.

He said nothing, just squinted out over the water, and she felt like a fool anyway.

Matt drove Kayla and Lloyd to the airport just as he'd promised. She'd called earlier and arranged for her and her father to take the same commuter plane to Fort Lauderdale. There they'd separate and go their respective ways. Matt waited for their flight with them, although Kayla failed to see why. He hardly spoke, keeping himself isolated behind a wall of aloofness, just as he'd been all morning.

When their flight was called, he walked with them outside to the small plane. Kayla felt uneasy, unsure what to do, how to say goodbye.

She told her father to go ahead, and when she and Matt stood alone on the heat-shimmering runway she simply did what came naturally. She gave him a spontaneous hug.

He backed away. "Don't." His expression was as stony as it had been the day she'd walked into his office. Was it only eight days ago? "Just get on the damn plane, Kayla," he snapped.

She nodded, swallowing her tears, before hurrying off to the waiting aircraft. Absurdly, the scene at the end of *Casablanca* flashed through her mind.

But of course this wasn't a movie and she didn't fade away with the credits. She flew to Chicago and resumed her life. She took apart her beaded braids, returned to work at the store, shared dinners with Frank, flew to San Francisco the next week.

While she was there she called her father and learned that Ruth had already come, settled her business affairs and gone back to Freeport. On Ruth's recommendation, Gordon and Kayla were to assume vice-president status, with a combined voice in the company equal to their father's. A sizable increase in salary accompanied the promotion, too.

"Oh, one other thing," her father added hesitantly. "I'm thinking of asking my payroll clerk, Margaret, to dinner some time. What do you think? Am I an old fool?"

"I think you should do what makes you happy, Dad."

A week passed, and then another. Kayla told herself she was following her own advice; she was doing what made her happy. But as the third week came to a close, she faced the somber fact that she was not happy. What she was was miserable.

She missed Matt more than she'd ever believed possible. She had thought each passing day would bring increasing release from the emotional hold he had on her, but she'd been wrong. If anything, it grew. She'd spent a mere week in his company and couldn't understand how this deep attachment had happened. Love involved so much more than what they'd shared. Or so she'd thought, but maybe she'd been wrong about that, too.

Missing Matt wasn't the only thing that made her unhappy those dreary, late-winter days. With increasing clarity, she saw her relationship with Frank for what it was, a comfortable convenience. They'd evolved into a dating couple simply because they traveled together, city to city. If she'd been settled in one place, she would have had the chance to meet other people. But given her lifestyle, Frank had seemed the only choice.

In addition, they shared a common knowledge and enthusiasm for the clockworks, which had led her to think they shared a lot more. But after being with Matt, after learning what being in love was really like, she knew she couldn't compromise herself, or Frank, by entering a passionless marriage. It wasn't fair to either of them.

There was one other reason she'd dated Frank, Kayla realized with deepening chagrin. He had Lloyd Brayton's stamp of approval. Her need to please her father had steered her into dating Frank just as insidiously as it had driven her to make a success of her stores.

During that last night on Grand Bahama, she and her father had talked about several important matters, but their relationship was not one of them. She wished they had, because this was not how she'd envisioned her life. She was not happy being a nomad, busy and successful though she was. She longed for roots; she missed Boston, missed the factory and, oh, how she missed being part of her family.

She was winding a reproduction Shaker wall clock in her showroom late on a Friday afternoon in mid-March when the realization hit her. All around her clocks were tick-tick-ticking, pendulums swinging ceaselessly, and for some unfathomable reason it just hit her. Life was passing her by. Kayla closed the bezel, sank into the nearest chair and simply broke down and cried.

That night she told Frank she wouldn't be seeing him outside of work anymore. He didn't take the news well, but she couldn't continue the charade that she loved him, and she certainly couldn't go on thinking they could share a happy marriage.

Two days later she flew home to Boston. Ruth and Philip had returned from the Bahamas a couple of weeks earlier, and when Kayla showed up on their doorstep asking if she could stay with them a few days, they were thrilled and said she could stay as long as she wanted.

The following evening Kayla met with her father, and though she was quaking in her boots, she forged ahead with her proposal. Lloyd would be disappointed in her. He'd think she was weak-spined for giving up the life she'd created, but she knew differently and, really, that was all that mattered. She finally believed that.

"You want to what?" He frowned, pouring a brandy. They were talking in his study at the house where she'd grown up. It had never felt like home to her, though, not the way her grandmother's place did.

"I want to move back to Boston, work at the factory."

"And what about your stores?"

"Let Frank manage them. He's more than qualified."

"But they're yours, your creation."

"Dad, listen." She clutched her hands tight, hesitating, anxious over his reaction. "I know you think I'm excess baggage around here and would prefer I stayed on the road. You have Gordon, and the two of you manage just fine. He's extremely capable—"

Lloyd lowered the crystal decanter slowly, carefully, his frown deepening.

"—but I'm tired of moving from one place to another, never staying long enough to make friends. And I'm definitely tired of playing catch-up." She lowered her eyes. "What I'm trying to say is, I'm sorry Mom died giving birth to me, but it wasn't my fault. I didn't will her to die, and I wish you'd stop treating me as if I had."

Lloyd Brayton's color drained until his face was ashen. "You think I . . . Oh, Kayla!" Numb, he dropped into a chair, brandy sloshing over his hand.

Lost in their respective heartache, they were silent for several long minutes.

"I'm sorry, Kayla," Lloyd finally said. "I didn't realize that was the message I was conveying. I'm really so sorry." Tears glistened in his eyes. "I guess I don't tell you often enough how proud I am of you. The courage you've shown by striking out on your own, your creativity—you amaze me, Kayla. I couldn't be prouder of you if I tried."

"Thank you. I appreciate your approval, but I really don't need it anymore. As I was saying, I want to give up that part of my life and come home. I'd prefer to work at the factory, but if there's no room for me there, I'll look for work elsewhere in Boston."

"No room for you!" Lloyd smiled, and the smile spread until he was laughing. "Honey, since your grandmother stopped working, we have room wider than the Grand Canyon. How soon can you start?"

Kayla relayed all this to Ruth the next morning over brioches and tea at the Ritz-Carlton, a new indulgence of Ruth's since her retirement. Ruth was thrilled, but when Kayla disclosed that she planned to fly straight back to Chicago that night to start dismantling her life there, she protested.

"Kayla, if you don't mind my saying so, you look awful—pale, run-down, emotionally depleted."

"Gee, thanks." Kayla smiled wryly.

"Heed my advice. Take some time off. Do something nice just for yourself." Ruth pressed her hand atop Kayla's. "Philip and I haven't said anything to your father yet. We're afraid he'll think we've really gone senile—" she chuckled "—but we bought the house we stayed at in the Bahamas."

"You *bought* it?"

"Uh-huh. It was a steal." Ruth winked. "A really smart investment, too. We won't have any trouble renting it when we're not there."

"You *bought* it?" Kayla was still stunned.

Ruth laughed. "Use it, Kayla. There's no one there for the next two weeks. Fly down and let yourself relax."

Kayla started to protest, but Ruth insisted. "Please. I'd be so happy if you did."

Kayla realized she did feel in need of some R and R. She hadn't been sleeping well, and her appetite was poor. And so she agreed. It was an impetuous decision, totally self-centered, and the guilt she suffered almost made her change her mind. But in the end, she went, arriving at the now familiar pink stucco airport late on a Thursday afternoon.

The first time she heard the musical phrase, "No problem, mon," spoken by a young baggage handler, her eyes misted. It was good to be back.

A taxi took her to the house, to the bright, breezy rooms, the fragrant garden and dazzling ocean beyond, and that brought tears to her eyes again. Still in her traveling clothes, she walked through the house and wandered the grounds, reacquainting herself with the property and the happy memories that dwelt here. The air was so thick with them, she almost believed she could feel Matt's presence.

She unpacked and after changing into the gauze dress she'd worn her last night here, she went down to the well-stocked kitchen and prepared a light supper. As the sun went down in a blaze of orange and pink, she decided to take a stroll up the beach.

It was dark by the time she returned. Kicking through the warm, gentle surf, she was reminded of the nights she and Matt had walked just so. Inevitably she wondered what he was doing at this moment, if he and his ex-wife were having dinner, if they'd progressed to the point of moving in together, and how soon it would be before they exchanged vows again. Had they already?

Her throat tightened at the thought and her vision blurred. Which was perfectly ridiculous. And reprehensible. Matt Reed belonged to someone else. She had no right to feel any which way about him.

But she did. She loved him and she missed him, and she didn't know how to stop.

She started up the beach toward the property gate, but then paused, drawn to enjoying the ocean view just a few minutes longer. Since she was here last, the moon had run its cycle and was again rising full, silvering the tips of the waves. From down the beach, from one of the large hotels, drifted the faint, dreamy sounds of a steel drum band. She sighed heavily, taking it all in.

Lights along the property fence behind her illuminated the beach where she stood, and with a soft intake of breath Kayla noticed how they cast her shadow down the sand and over the curling waves. She fought against the memory, but the image of her and Matt casting their shadows just so overtook her anyway.

She closed her eyes tight, riding out a wave of pure, unadulterated grief. Perhaps she'd been wrong to come back to this place. Everything she looked at, everything she heard, smelled, tasted, felt, was imbued with memories of Matt. As long as she was here, she'd never stop thinking about him.

Exhaling, she slowly opened her eyes—and then snapped them wide open. She blinked, blinked again, but the shadow was still there, a second shadow alongside hers. On a surge of adrenaline and mindless hope, she spun around. And there he was.

"Hello, Kayla."

"Matt?" she asked, thinking he might be a figment of her imagination.

"Yes. Hello."

She studied his face, let her hungry gaze roam over his tall, solid frame, devouring every inch of him. "What are you doing here?"

He came closer, until she caught the intoxicating scent of him. "Ruth phoned me after you made the decision to come here. She suggested I join you."

Kayla's pulse was racing. "You're staying here, too?"

"Yes. I arrived yesterday, but I thought I'd go off today, let you settle in and be alone for a while."

"This doesn't make sense." Kayla passed a shaky hand over her brow. "Why on earth would my grandmother arrange for us to be here alone together?"

"Why?" In the moonlight she saw a faint smile curl over Matt's lips as he moved closer. "This is why," he whispered, holding her lightly by the shoulders and pulling her forward. And then he kissed her.

She thought to protest, even made a halfhearted attempt to back away, but his arms encircled her, and her conviction wavered. It felt too glorious to be in his embrace again. The next moment he deepened the kiss and she melted into a pool of responsiveness.

When he finally lifted his head, she was fighting for breath. "Matt, this can't happen."

"Why not?" His left eyebrow curled. She thought she'd never get tired of that delightful quirk.

"Because." She squirmed away from his hold and tucked her long, flowing hair behind her ears.

"Because what?"

"Don't play dense, Matthew. Are you, or are you not, reconciling with your ex-wife?"

He looked thunderstruck. "Is that what this is all about?"

"Answer me. When we flew down here last month, were you and Candace exploring the possibility of reuniting?"

"Yes, we were."

His answer tore at her. "Well, then."

"Listen, Kayla, she came to me with the idea, I didn't go to her, and the only reason she did was because she isn't doing as well financially as she'd expected when we split, and I am. All she was interested in was her own welfare and comfort. Of course I didn't realize that at first. I believed she sincerely wanted to make a go of our marriage, and, well, I felt obliged to at least talk about it and consider the possibility."

He would, Kayla thought. Matt was a man of honor, and a vow made was a vow kept.

"But it was a preposterous idea. Our marriage was a mistake right from the beginning. We were too young when we got married, too different. The only thing she and I ever did right was to separate. Time apart hasn't changed anything, either. We still want different things out of life, and we still get on each other's nerves, big time. No, Kayla, there's no love lost between me and Candace."

Kayla's mouth had fallen open; she was speechless. With an effort she stammered, "But... but what about all those times I caught you deep in thought? The week we spent here, so often you seemed troubled, as if you were thinking about something really serious."

"I was." He smiled gently, smoothing her hair. "I was bothered by the fact that I was falling in love with you, and I didn't know how to handle it."

The earth tilted at his words and began to spin. His smile broadened and glittered in his eyes. Kayla was sure the only thing keeping her from floating away was his hold on her, his hands lightly framing her face.

"You were... falling in love? With me?"

"Hook, line and sinker." He leaned in and brushed his lips across hers. His breath, when he laughed, mingled with hers. "But I didn't want to be in love. You were right when you said I was afraid of getting seriously involved because I'd been hurt by my divorce. You were right again about that being the reason I made work my top priority."

"Why didn't you say something? Why did you let me leave without telling me?"

Matt became thoughtful. "Fear wasn't the only reason I didn't want to get involved with you, Kayla. After you told me about your career and your...your ten-year plan, I realized how different we were on a very basic level. I know I told you Candace was right not to want children and a house in the suburbs, but those things were important to me eight years ago and, I'm sorry, but they still are now, maybe more so, since I'm that much older."

"But—"

He placed a finger gently over her lips. "I thought you deserved better, someone who could at least cope with your career, let you live the life you chose and not give you a hard time about it. I saw disaster on our horizon—differing aspirations, arguments and eventually failure. And it would be my fault once again, a direct repetition of what I went through with Candace."

"*That's* why you didn't stop me from returning to Chicago?"

Matt nodded. "That, and what you said about our week together. You dismissed it so casually, I was convinced it meant nothing to you."

Kayla shook her head. What a pair of fools they made! "So why are you here now?" she asked.

"Ruth phoned and told me about your decision to move back to Boston. That gave me hope that I might be wrong." He pulled her closer and fit his body to hers. Kayla drew in a sharp breath at the glorious contact.

"Not that it mattered," he continued, brushing kisses down the side of her face. "I'd already made a decision of my own. I'd finally decided I could put up with anything—ten-year plans, a house without kids, long absences when you were on the road—as long as I knew I'd have you with me part of the time. If you'd have me, that is."

Kayla's heart rate accelerated. Was he saying what she thought he was saying?

"I couldn't stop thinking about you, Kayla. The idea of you being with another man drove me crazy. This past month has been the worst in my life." He stroked her spine and she shivered with pleasure, even while tears formed in her eyes.

"It's been horrible for me, too, Matt. But you realize, don't you, that kids and dogs and picket fences are just as important to me as they are to you?"

Matt tilted his head, studying her cautiously.

"It was easy to postpone those things when I was going out with Frank. That's because I didn't love him. I didn't really want those things with him."

Hope flickered through Matt's expression. "And?"

"And I realized that once you find the right man, those things become very desirable. Maybe even urgent."

"And?" he urged again, his eyes glinting brighter.

"And I've found the right man."

He folded her against him, his eyes pressing shut. "I thought you'd never notice," he whispered against her hair.

"Never notice! Oh, Matt, I love you so much it hurts."

He lifted his head to gaze at her.

"And I love you, Kayla. With all my heart, with all my soul, I love you." He kissed her then, a tender kiss that spoke of promises and the future.

With his mouth still drifting across hers, he whispered, "The only question that remains is, how soon will you marry me?"

Kayla laughed, snuggling into his hardness and warmth. "Do you mean it?"

"Kayla, Kayla. Since that mess-up a month ago, I promised myself to never again say anything I don't mean."

"Well, then, how about as soon as possible?"

"Sounds good to me. Where?"

"Here. At the Garden of the Groves, like Gran and your father."

Matt lifted her off her feet. "You've got yourself a deal, Ms. Brayton." He spun her till she was dizzy.

Setting her down, he smiled playfully. "I lied. I have one more question for you, Kayla. Purely hypothetical, of course," he added with elaborate dryness. "What are your feelings on beginning a honeymoon before a wedding?"

"Hmm." She rubbed her chin, thinking. "I'm not sure. I can't think hypothetically at the moment. I'm afraid I need hands-on field experience to make that decision."

Laughing, Matt pressed a kiss to the top of her head. "Kayla Brayton, this could be the beginning of a beautiful life."

"Count on it, Matthew. Count on it."

With their arms linked and their happiness overflowing, they started toward the house.

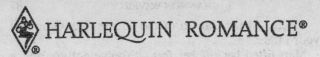

HARLEQUIN ROMANCE®

Coming Next Month

#3383 THE MARRIAGE RISK Debbie Macomber
The second book in Midnight Sons, a very special new six-book series from this bestselling author.

Welcome to Hard Luck, Alaska. Population: 150—mostly men! Location: north of the Arctic Circle. And meet the O'Halloran brothers, who run a bush-plane service called Midnight Sons. They're also heading a campaign to attract women to their town....

In *The Marriage Risk*, Charles O'Halloran, the oldest brother, finally decides to take a chance on marriage. But there's something he doesn't know about Lanni Caldwell, the woman he's fallen in love with—something important.

#3384 CHARLOTTE'S COWBOY Jeanne Allan
Charlotte Darnelle wanted to make one thing clear—she was not a redhead. She was a strawberry blonde, and any man who thought otherwise was in deep trouble. Needless to say, rancher Matthew Thornton was in it up to his Stetson!

#3385 SISTER SECRET Jessica Steele
Family Ties
Belvia had been trying to protect her painfully shy twin, Josy, from the attentions of Latham Tavenner, and now he thought she was a loose woman—deserving of his contempt! Belvia couldn't afford to alienate him—the family firm badly needed his financial support. So how long would it be before Latham took advantage...?

#3386 UNDERCOVER LOVER Heather Allison
Sealed with a Kiss
There was no room for sentiment in the newspaper business. And certainly no room at all for the blistering attraction Kate Brandon felt for Maxwell Hunter! The celebrated photographer might have come to her rescue once, but she couldn't, wouldn't, fraternize with a man she was competing with to get an exclusive picture. And as for falling in love...

AVAILABLE THIS MONTH:

#3379 BRIDES FOR BROTHERS
Debbie Macomber

#3380 THE BEST MAN
Shannon Waverly

#3381 ONCE BURNED
Margaret Way

#3382 LEGALLY BINDING
Jessica Hart

MILLION DOLLAR SWEEPSTAKES (III)

No purchase necessary. To enter, follow the directions published. Method of entry may vary. For eligibility, entries must be received no later than March 31, 1996. No liability is assumed for printing errors, lost, late or misdirected entries. Odds of winning are determined by the number of eligible entries distributed and received. Prizewinners will be determined no later than June 30, 1996.

Sweepstakes open to residents of the U.S. (except Puerto Rico), Canada, Europe and Taiwan who are 18 years of age or older. All applicable laws and regulations apply. Sweepstakes offer void wherever prohibited by law. Values of all prizes are in U.S. currency. This sweepstakes is presented by Torstar Corp., its subsidiaries and affiliates, in conjunction with book, merchandise and/or product offerings. For a copy of the Official Rules send a self-addressed, stamped envelope (WA residents need not affix return postage) to: MILLION DOLLAR SWEEPSTAKES (III) Rules, P.O. Box 4573, Blair, NE 68009, USA.

EXTRA BONUS PRIZE DRAWING

No purchase necessary. The Extra Bonus Prize will be awarded in a random drawing to be conducted no later than 5/30/96 from among all entries received. To qualify, entries must be received by 3/31/96 and comply with published directions. Drawing open to residents of the U.S. (except Puerto Rico), Canada, Europe and Taiwan who are 18 years of age or older. All applicable laws and regulations apply; offer void wherever prohibited by law. Odds of winning are dependent upon number of eligible entries received. Prize is valued in U.S. currency. The offer is presented by Torstar Corp., its subsidiaries and affiliates in conjunction with book, merchandise and/or product offering. For a copy of the Official Rules governing this sweepstakes, send a self-addressed, stamped envelope (WA residents need not affix return postage) to: Extra Bonus Prize Drawing Rules, P.O. Box 4590, Blair, NE 68009, USA.

SWP-H1095

Become a Privileged Woman,
You'll be entitled to all these Free Benefits. And Free Gifts, too.

To thank you for buying our books, we've designed an exclusive FREE program called *PAGES & PRIVILEGES™*. You can enroll with just one Proof of Purchase, and get the kind of luxuries that, until now, you could only read about.

BIG HOTEL DISCOUNTS

A privileged woman stays in the finest hotels. And so can you—at up to 60% off! Imagine standing in a hotel check-in line and watching as the guest in front of you pays $150 for the same room that's only costing you $60. Your *Pages & Privileges* discounts are good at Sheraton, Marriott, Best Western, Hyatt and thousands of other fine hotels all over the U.S., Canada and Europe.

FREE DISCOUNT TRAVEL SERVICE

A privileged woman is always jetting to romantic places. When you fly, just make one phone call for the lowest published airfare at time of booking—or double the difference back!

BONUS
Proof of Purchase
Offer expires October 31, 1996

PLUS—you'll get a $25 voucher to use the first time you book a flight AND 5% cash back on every ticket you buy thereafter through the travel service!

PROOF OF PURCHASE
Offer expires October 31, 1996

HR-PP6B